W9-DIO-771

MW

10-11

UNINVITED

JAMES GABRIEL BERMAN

WARNER BOOKS

A Time Warner Company

Warner Books, Inc., 1271 Avenue of the Americas, New York, NY 10020

W A Time Warner Company

Printed in the United States of America
First Printing: April 1995
10 9 8 7 6 5 4 3 2 1

Library of Congress Cataloging-in-Publication Data

Berman, James Gabriel.
    Uninvited / James Gabriel Berman.
        p.   cm.
    ISBN 0-446-51861-1
    I. Trials (Murder)—United States—Fiction.   I. Title.
PS3552.E72497U55   1995
813' .54—dc20   94-19748
                                                   CIP

Book design by Giorgetta Bell McRee

For my parents

In acknowledgment of those who are always invited:

Barbara Zitwer, Karen Kelly, Larry Kirshbaum,
Marlene Adelstein, María Lamadrid,
Nina Davenport, Ethan Herschenfeld, Ron Berenson,
George Lombardi, Teri Kaplan,
Cummington Community of the Arts.

What beck'ning ghost, along the moonlight shade
Invites my steps, and points to yonder glade?

—ALEXANDER POPE,
"Elegy to the Memory of an Unfortunate Lady"

UNINVITED

Prelude

It wasn't much—at least, at first. It didn't make the front page of the *New York Post* or get a contract for a TV miniseries. Initially, it didn't make a stir west of Garden City. It wasn't the prime breakfast conversation at the Acropolis Diner on Northern Boulevard. There they talked about the Islanders, property taxes and unemployment. Manhattan cabbies weren't too keen on it. The Long Island Railroad conductors didn't chat it up between tickets. No school declared a day of mourning on its account. Few mothers would warn their children as a result of it. Still fewer preachers would declaim about it from their pulpits that Sunday.

In quieter places it would've fed journalists for weeks, but here on Long Island there was a lot of competition: There'd been a gang rape in Glen Cove that claimed a young girl's life that Saturday, a serial killer was on the loose preying on teenage boys, a crack-addict carjacker had made headlines by requiring his victims to pray for him, a Vietnam vet had gone berserk on an overdose, an accountant had cremated his lover, a rabid dog had crossed from Suffolk to Nassau County.

After all, an overworked businessman who'd done away with his kids and wife and then himself was almost part of the suburban rhythm—like little league or PTA luncheons. You couldn't have made it interesting, even in fiction, and so it was pushed to the second page. There were no leads. The police had declared it murder-suicide.

The details were banal enough: morbid, but all too familiar. Four bodies, those of the Carver family, discovered in their expansive home, in very exclusive Hautucket Bay. No sign of forced entry. The kids, aged two and five, each shot cleanly through the head. The boy had been killed in his bedroom, under the covers, having been tucked in. The daughter in the bathroom, on the toilet, her underwear pulled down to her ankles. At first they thought she might have been sexually abused, which would've given the case new life, but nothing ever came of that. The mother, aged twenty-seven, was discovered in the kitchen. She'd been warming up old Chinese food in the microwave for a midnight snack. Her spinal cord was punctured by a bullet to the abdomen.

Meanwhile, the much older father (fifty-six that June) was in his study. He'd shot himself in the temple as a curtain call. He was still holding the pistol, a .38 revolver, when the police arrived. It was found gripped loosely in his right hand.

So that was it. What they call anywhere—not just in Long Island—an open-and-shut case. And outside of Hautucket, no one paused to think much of it. In town, however, was another matter. From the working-class enclave of Porter Hill that serviced all the estates to the Crescent Lochs Country Club where not a Jew or a Black was yet to set foot, it was the only thing on anyone's mind. Although greater Long Island was well used to violence, Hautucket, the prim and proper town, the bastion of Gold Coast values and thick portfolios, where Mercedes and Land Rovers ferried kids to school with nannies at the wheel, was not.

The last murder had been a domestic incident—one which the community had disposed of as a drunken spat turned bloody. But for six years this perfect community had complacently waved to its eight-man police force, left its doors unlocked (albeit with the security gates closed), sent its children trick-or-treating on Halloween, sponsored bake sales and quietly occupied itself with opposing the busing in of "wrong types."

Of course, everyone knew of a marriage or two in divorce court, a coke-addict son, an anorexic daughter, a mastiff with worms, a real estate developer laid low by the recession, an incestuous uncle, a mastectomy malpracticed, a stock option ungranted, a tennis match rained out, or a divorcée who was having one too many on the cocktail circuit. Hautucket accepted its shortcomings, not that it advertised them—but it could handle the privileges and burdens of wealth with somnolent sangfroid and puritanical closed lips.

But a whole family wiped out? That was a matter for soul-searching. Not that there would be any. The day after the deaths were discovered, the police department immediately found itself strong-armed by spin doctors, a group of town elders who made it their business to keep the wraps on what had quickly become Hautucket's dirty little secret. This, as much as the Long Islander's jaded spirit, accounted for the lack of greater media attention. Within hours the police department had issued a statement that the case was closed—a despondent father and an unlucky family, nothing more, nothing less—a regrettable incident.

So the outside world dismissed it. A producer for a talk show made one feeble inquiry but quickly lost interest and instead bid for the rights to the gang rape in Merrick. Hautucket shuttered up its windows and breathed an inaudible sigh of relief. At least there wouldn't be too many TV crews racing to the schools to question friends of the deceased children. There were some interviews, mostly by local affiliates, but then they tapered off.

In the Hollow, the wealthiest section of Hautucket, where houses go for a million, there was no talk at all. Probably, because there was no one to talk to. With four-acre zoning and gates marking the driveways, the concept of neighbor takes on new meaning. Sometimes neighbors can almost be in different zip codes. Sometimes, neighbors only see one another at the club, and then drive back in their separate cars. This was the land of once endless estates, many of them now subdivided—the neck of the woods in which Jay Gatsby had thrown his lavish parties— the once grand Gold Coast, now past its heyday, but still the richest county per capita in the United States. So most talk occurred at board meetings and fundraisers. There wasn't any need for any other kind of talk. But it was surprising that there was so little talk in the Hollow because the Hollow was where the Carvers had lived. And although their neighbors had rarely heard them speak, or sing, or drive into the garage, or play, they did hear the gunshots that night.

Their house wasn't visible from the road, and aside from the unmarked police cruiser standing guard at the base of the winding gravel driveway, there was no sign of anything amiss. The Carvers had recently installed new fencing—a stone wall really—that some Hollow residents had objected to. But soon they backed off because no one really wanted to litigate. The value of the property, beautiful and well maintained, had been assessed at $2.3 million the prior tax year. Mrs. Carver had done a series of lush plantings along the gravel drive that snaked via a charming wooden bridge over a small creek and past the carriage house. The main building, sprawling and Victorian, with a view of the bay from three exposures, would have been the envy of many a family, but in Hautucket it was just another nice home. From his study window on the third floor, Mr. Carver used to like watching the boats in the bay on a clear summer evening. He would take a scotch, neat, and seat himself at his desk—he never had liked to recline except while sleeping, thinking it decadent, and had maintained that sitting up straight is a virtue close to godliness. It was part of his effort to fit into Hautucket Bay's values. His children would have grown to know the lecture well.

So not much of anything was discussed in the Hollow. Few people had really known the Carvers anyway. Mr. Carver had been shunned by the highest social set in Hautucket, because his family hadn't been in the community for enough generations. He'd made his money crassly for these parts—by acquiring control of one of the largest networks of BMW dealerships in the Northeast. He'd moved to the North Shore from Hartford and within a few years had established a few successful dealerships. It wasn't long before he was telling BMW how to run its northeast operations. His past was a mystery, and mysteries of that sort don't go over that well in Hautucket society. And his wife? No one really knew her past. Of course, they suspected the worst. Even so, the Carvers were eventually granted a membership in the Crescent Lochs Club—and then at the Blue Hill Winter Club, an exclusive skating rink with a six-year waiting list—after some muted reluctance. They were, however, routinely passed over for most social gatherings.

In the Hollow, however, there were theories about the killings. Mostly whispered; rarely spoken. The husbands thought Carver had merely had a few dry years like the rest of Long Island and that his business had been ready to file for bankruptcy. Anyone in these parts was less than understanding about those who didn't come from such old money that it didn't really matter how business was. Here, solidity was the virtue, and bankruptcy was seen as the just deserts for up-and-comers, speculators and the nouveau riche of any sort. If Carver's business had problems, they must have been of his own making—the result of being overextended or overleveraged. In other words, greed, that cardinal sin among old-money Protestants, was to blame.

R. Todd Chilton III was of this opinion. An executive vice-president of a giant pharmaceuticals concern, Chilton was also the scion of a very wealthy family dating itself back to the *Mayflower.* Bold and irreverent for his type and profession, he still had no soft spot for whatever troubles Carver may have been in. Very few of his set even felt comfortable discussing the Carver incident, but Chilton was different in that way. Between canapés and consommé at a dinner party one night, he mentioned that Carver had probably wanted to turn to one of them—he indicated the assembled group of guests—but laughed that Carver must have owed all of them money. Everyone laughed uneasily at this suggestion, for each had given him something. But none wished to admit that they'd invested in anything so low-class as a string of car dealerships.

The wives spoke differently about things. To them, it

was probably a marital problem, a case of a mistress or a lover discovered. Money problems may have loaded the gun, but deeper quandaries, those of the heart, pulled the trigger. No one had any firsthand information. No one knew the mystery man. There were speculations, but nothing much came of it. Lara Fayerweather had an all-too-titillating idea—only mentioned in the Crescent Lochs powder room—that Patricia Carver had been leading a double life all her days, with a Moroccan prince who'd finally declared an ultimatum. There were even a few takers to this theory, for you could have believed it. Patricia Carver had been beautiful and glamorous. And then there was that age difference. But after a few rounds, the story died out. No Moroccan prince had shown up. And it didn't look likely that one would.

In fact, the Carvers were not so cosmopolitan as fantasy suggested. They had been homebodies—such an unusual trait for people of such means that they'd felt compelled to explain it. It was often said that Mrs. Carver hated planes, and only traveled by car or train—with the one exception of the Concorde, which because of its quiet engine, she could endure. But royalty had never courted Patricia Carver, and it never would.

Across town, in Porter Hill, people had different ideas. The killings were, in contrast to Long Island at large and the Hollow locally, popular topics there. In the pubs, pool halls, and cigarette shops, everyone had a theory. Porter Hill was to the Hollow what Harlem was to Fifth Avenue: a zone of low rents and laundry lines—a ready supply of cheap labor whose proximity was tolerated because of its usefulness. Porter Hill residents were by no means revolutionaries. They devoted little time to thinking about inequities. The paychecks came in, and they were grateful. Realism was their creed, not ideology. The rich they looked at with suspicion, sometimes envy, but mostly with awe. They were honest enough to admit that that's what they wanted eventually, and some of them had even gotten rich after getting out.

About the Carver killings most Porter Hill people were cynical or superstitious, but strangely more sympathetic. Instead of being contemptuous of his excesses, they figured Mr. Carver had been doing something all of them had done on a small scale from time to time: taken from the till. At Killian's Pub on March Street, Killian himself was spreading the rumor that Carver had been stealing from the dealerships for years and had finally been snitched on. Kimball Killian, a squat, mustached man with a voice of pure gravel, insisted to whoever would listen that Carver had operated things with a massive Ponzi scheme that had fallen on top of itself. He said that Carver hadn't sold a car in years, but had managed to cook the books. A few disciples took to Killian's theory, until one remembered that there'd been a news story exactly like that a year earlier, of a car dealer who'd been arrested for playing those games. After that, Killian lost his disciples and went back to doling out whiskey and beer.

Around the corner, at Vincent's, a seafood dive that specializes in fried clams and Budweiser on tap, everyone was bragging that Carver had once come in for takeout a few years back. Nearly every vendor or delivery boy claimed to have a Carver story, about approaching the dark house and having sensed danger through the tall trees and across the sloping lawn of the property—even then.

At the post office, Carl Hughson, the longtime mail sorter for the Hollow, did little to dismiss the notion that he'd been privy to inside information. He told a co-worker that he'd noticed some "strange things" posted to the Carver house in the days before the killings. When pressed on it, he'd say he couldn't talk about it—the police would want the information eventually—and he was compelled to keep quiet until then. Everyone knew Hughson had a history of mental imbalance and so they humored him, constantly reminding him not to forget what those strange things were—to write them down. In reality, Hughson would never have to say anything, not because he'd forgotten whatever it was he had to keep close to his heart, but because the police never asked.

Yet, Detective Lyle McDonough of the Nassau County Special Homicide Squad, a new unit set up to deal with the proliferation of Long Island murder cases, was getting curious. He did feel like asking some questions—perhaps not to Carl Hughson—but maybe to the Carvers' maid, or to the myriad of business associates with whom Kirk Carver had had dealings. When McDonough called the Hautucket police department, he got a cool response. The last thing Hautucket wanted was an outside unit getting involved in their jurisdiction. But McDonough wouldn't back off so easily. He'd been given leeway to investigate any homicide in Nassau County. And a week ago, he'd been reprimanded by his supervisor and castrated by the press for botching a confession. McDonough needed the big one. So he looked at Hautucket and saw his suburban oyster—among the beautiful homes and monied lifestyles. There had to be something else out there—something hiding among those quiet cul-de-sacs and impressive bay views. McDonough decided to find it.

Maybe a month before R. Todd Chilton would be toasting to murders and mergers both, Kimball Killian serving up gossip and ale from the same tap, Lara Fayerweather chatting with the ladies about distinctly unladylike things, Carl Hughson sorting out fantasies from third-class fliers, and Lyle McDonough struggling to cull a career from the crimes of others, a young man in a yellow windbreaker was reading the paper with no particular interest.

The white shirt under his jacket was filthy from his shift waiting tables. Exhausted, he'd come to the Porter Hill Diner, where he could sit back and be served himself. It was past three in the morning and the diner was the only thing open in town. May came along with the coffee. She waddled over the same way she always did, order pad tucked in waistband, three sticks of gum snapping away in her jaw.

"Hon, you're in later than usual. You slaving away over there?"

"No, May, a flat. I spent at least an hour and a half changing it."

"Poor Tony baby. Always a problem in your backyard, right hon?"

Tony McMahon, christened Antonio Grasso McMahon, aged way before his time by a mother who'd died young and by a father who refused to die at all, sat and sipped. He wasn't much interested in the paper that evening. Usually, he'd just look up the Islanders' scores anyway. Sometimes he'd read some of the sordid stories that took up the first few pages.

He sat back and signaled for more coffee. He could catch at least six hours' sleep before he'd have to go to his lunch shift. Normally, he wouldn't have had so much coffee this late if he had to catch quick sleep and work a shift so soon after, but he still had a fifteen-minute drive home to his apartment in Glen River.

May put the radio on, all ads and static. An announcer issued a bulletin: The Carver family of Hautucket Bay had been discovered dead after a neighbor heard gunshots. No further details. May went back to her station to write up a couple of checks. She couldn't have cared less about such a thing. Mass murders and sickly stories were really no one's rightful business. Besides, if she listened she'd never get to sleep—what, with her edema and her bad dreams. But she'd heard the Carver name before. She knew it'd made it-

self familiar somehow, the way radio ad jingles root themselves cruelly in the brain.

"Ain't that the guy who owns the car showrooms up on
Hugenot? Jesus, I think that's it. I probably pass that damn
sign every day and never've given it a moment's thought.
Sure, Carver BMW, that's it. I wonder if it's the same family.
Sad thing."

Tony wasn't listening to May. If he had, he would've
been able to confirm her suspicions. It was indeed the same
family—the family of that BMW dealership and a dozen
more. Not that May would know any of the others. She
rarely traveled out of Porter Hill.

But Tony knew the name and the family both. He didn't
know them from the billboards or the BMW showrooms.
He didn't know them from delivering Chinese food to the
house or from gossip overheard in a country club. He didn't
know them from sorting their mail in the post office. Nor
did he know them from business partnerships or little
league or mowing their lawn. He knew the Carver family
of Locust Lane in one way only: for though he'd certainly
never been a Moroccan prince, he had loved Patricia
Carver.

May wished him a good night, but he didn't hear. He
was thinking about the Carvers. He hadn't said so to May,
of course, but he figured Patricia Carver had deserved it. As
he saw it, if it hadn't been that night, it would've been another. For Patricia had always been bad news.

Always.

From the very earliest days. And bad news begets bad news. At least that's how he saw it.

He opened the diner door. It was drizzling, so he turned up the collar on his windbreaker. He listened. It was silent at this hour. A car or two you could hear from the thruway, but not much more. He buttoned up and crumpled the rest of his wages into his pocket. Yes, bad news begets bad news, he thought. There was no question about that.

1

If you follow the coastal road in Hautucket Bay long enough, you'll hit the neighboring community of Fisher's Cove. And if you turn right at Belmont Street and follow that all the way to the highway, you'll cross into Glen River, once a middle-class community of small, tidy homes and well-tended lawns. If you've seen an ad from the fifties for a lawnmower, with a smiling dad on the front lawn displaying his trusty machine, you might as well have seen the old Glen River. It was quintessential suburbia—not the haughty mega-acreage of the Hollow, nor the row houses of Porter Hill—but a collection of humble mortgages and sturdy pensions, decent jobs and the best intentions. It was an ordinary community. And, like any other ordinary community, far from perfect—despite appearances.

Glen River had become a symbol of Long Island's prosperity in the glory years. No one was without a livelihood and hope for success. Every family had a big enough lot to put on an addition when another kid came along. Every garage was two-car. The schools were good enough and the taxes reasonable.

Then things changed: The recession came. Glen River never really recovered. Fathers lost jobs. Mothers went into the workplace only to find thin wages. Homeowners defaulted on loans. Alcoholics Anonymous groups popped up like McDonald's franchises. Immigrants poured into the community, taking advantage of lower real estate prices and buying cheap. Their success bred resentment among the older residents. Tensions mounted. The schools fell apart. Metal detectors were installed at the doors. Gangs of unemployed youths terrorized the Portuguese, the Haitians, the Asians—and anyone else with a strange last name.

Tony had spent those days drifting across the country, working odd jobs. Now he was enrolled in Community College at Hicksville. He worked part time at the Anchor 'n Sail, an inland seafood spot that, always one step away from failing a health inspection, sat not too far from the train tracks in Syosset.

It was from the Anchor 'n Sail that Tony was driving on that warm spring day exactly six months and one day after the Carver killings. He turned on the radio. Happy with the music and the breeze and the end of the lunch shift, he rolled down his window. It had been a rotten winter with more snow than usual for the Island and everyone had been longing for spring. Now that it had finally arrived, people were starting to sit on stoops and inhabit the parks.

It was a quick ride back to Glen River, where he'd fixed up the garage off his father's house into a small studio flat. He'd installed a sink and toilet and purchased a hot plate, toaster-oven and small fridge. For showers he still had to cross through the main house, often past his father, passed out on the couch. But most of the time he was comfortable there. Even though his father hadn't worked in years, scraping together less food and more booze from his disability wages, he was rarely awake long enough to bother Tony. And he'd barely lifted his head from the sofa when Tony'd returned home after being gone for years.

So he was looking forward to getting back to his garage apartment, washing up, and having a beer out on the lawn chair. At the intersection of Belmont and King streets, he turned left and that's when he noticed it. At first, you wouldn't think much of it, would you? A gray sedan behind you in broad daylight, turning where you turn, stopping where you stop, yielding where you yield? But after two or three turns that he had to make anyway and then three or four others that were for the sake of the gray sedan, he began to worry. Besides, he was accustomed to being doubtful of anyone and everything.

What happened next he would always remember, not the thoughts during it, but strange, almost subliminal sensations: the shouts of the arresting officer, the metallic feel of his own car's hood as he was frisked, the painful pressure on his arms to squeeze them into the cuffs, the awkwardness of his imprisoned march across the pavement, the urine scent of the back seat of the squad car, the rhythmic chanting of the Miranda rights that echoed in his ear.

He'd always figured he'd end up in jail, but he wasn't sure how. Everyone who knew him would have said that Tony McMahon lived his life governed by what pop psychologists call paranoid delusions—what the rest of us might call crazy thoughts. For a period of time when he was out of school and out of work, he'd devoted his time to concocting conspiracy theories about his neighbors, his father, old friends and passersby. He'd once visited an electronic surveillance store and walked out with four hundred dollars' worth of gadgets meant to secure his safety: phone-tap foilers, motion detectors, a two-way mirror, a book on corporate security techniques. Around that time he'd also subscribed to a few questionable magazines published for espionage buffs with names like *Deadly Intruder* and *Tactics of Revenge.* What he was protecting himself against, he wasn't exactly sure. But over the years, he always had one deadly intruder or another in mind. Once, when he thought his father was stealing from him, he'd booby-trapped his money tin with a small bomb—a homemade contraption made from an M-80 explosive, a cigarette lighter and a mousetrap. After weeks of his dad still walking around with ten fingers, Tony discovered it to be a dud.

He'd bought a .38 Smith & Wesson, a model 10 military and police revolver with a three-inch barrel, a common big gun, that he'd gone awhile keeping always under his jean jacket. With the tail end of his savings, he'd installed a surveillance camera that loomed oddly on the corner of the garage. He'd often squandered an afternoon watching the activity in front of the house: the children on tricycles, the newspaper deliveries, the plumbing calls, the housewives returning with their mall purchases—never a thug, never an avenger.

Finally, he'd feared the inexplicable. In this group he included everyone—the postman, rodents, Manhattanites, reporters, his father's sister, Girl Scouts hawking cookies, salesmen, and finally police. So he always lived his life wary of blue-and-white cars. Today was no different than any other day.

He'd expected to be picked up anyway as soon as he'd heard of the Carver killings. He knew they'd eventually question the idea that Kirk Carver had killed himself. Therefore, it was just a matter of routine and time before they'd come to arrest a murder suspect. And he never ever doubted that he'd be the first one hauled in. He'd only been surprised that it had taken so long.

He said nothing as the magistrate read the charge—four counts of first degree murder among other, gentler things—and echoed the pre-set bail determination from the arrest warrant: Denied. The magistrate announced the denial without expression, popped a glycerin tablet and announced the date of Antonio Grasso McMahon's arraignment. Once Tony had glanced at the assistant prosecutor—he'd shown up late—a young clean-shaven guy with a stuffed briefcase, but the DA didn't look back.

Then he was thrown back into a cruiser to be transported to the county correctional. By now some local press had smelled a story and a few reporters were there on the steps to snap photos and ask questions. He made no attempt to hide his face. Silent, he watched the assembled watchers. He felt no shame or worry. A defense mechanism that he'd had since very young—a protection he'd honed early to defend himself against the disgraces of a sadistic father and the impotence of a sickly mother—allowed him to set his consciousness and his emotions on different clocks so that the one ran way ahead of the other. As if in a different time zone, his thoughts dealt with things before his feelings.

Finally, he was behind bars and he sat on the spare, padded bench that was a bed. He was thankful for having a cell to himself, not realizing he'd been given one because he'd been classified as potentially violent. He checked out the dimensions. 8' x 12'. He could estimate it in an instant. That was a talent left over from his contracting days. Ninety-six square feet didn't seem too bad to him at all. He only had 225 at home anyway. He laughed aloud. So that was the difference between captivity and freedom, he thought smugly: 129 lousy feet. He felt like shouting it out to the world—that that was all they were working toward with their consciences and good deeds, with their nine-to-five jobs and church services on Sunday, with their volunteer work and social welfare, with their moral sermonizing and nonprofit lobbying: 129 lousy feet.

He turned on the faucet. It worked. He flushed the toilet. That worked too. No shower, of course. He'd heard plenty of stories about communal prison showers. He'd never been in one, but he'd be prepared. For he'd had a year of tai-kwon-do. The cell next to his was empty, but he saw a guy sleeping two doors down. He lay on his own hard bed and started to dream.

He remembered a feeling he'd had long ago when a girl had touched his arm. It was a good feeling, powerful, not sexual—chilling. He'd kissed her then and smelled her perfume, a rich, sophisticated scent that she'd always bragged was from a faraway land, not Glen River or even Calabria, where her grandparents were from, but from somewhere beyond, a place unticketed. He rolled in the narrow, uncomfortable bed with the pleasure of the unconscious memory. The girl now kissed him on the forehead, played with his hair, breathed on his fingers, laid her head on his stomach. She then left to go shopping and he knew, in the way that lovers know, that she would return. But she didn't.

Then he woke up to the cell and cried. His separate clocks, the one of consciousness and the other of feeling, had inescapably wound together.

He recalled a play he'd read in school—one he'd only half understood. There was a line he'd scribbled in his yearbook so as not to forget it because it had struck him so: *When I waked, I cried to dream again.* He remembered it now and said it over and over. He counted the words in it, then the syllables, then the letters, for he had a mania for counting things. But after a while, maybe ten minutes, he grew tired of it and banged his head once against the wall so that blood trickled down onto the small, uncased pillow.

2

Nearly two decades earlier, while a much younger R. Todd Chilton III was summering at private beaches on Fire Island, and the Killian family was contenting themselves with a dip in the Porter Hill community pool, a pretty but awkward little girl was putting her big toe into the water at Jones Beach. She grimaced at the surprising cold of it. Then she squealed as her brother who, witnessing her discomfort and not being one to miss such an opportunity, splashed her with the salty surf. The water wouldn't get really warm until later in the summer, for it was only Memorial Day.

The little girl tried to get back at her brother the only way she knew how: telling on him. But their mother, who was busy sunbathing and not to be disturbed, ignored the yelling and accusations. So the little girl was left on her own. She quickly forgot about her brother and went back to the sandcastle she'd constructed.

It was a complex castle—a good job by any ten-year-old's standards—one with underground passages and bucket-molded turrets that guarded against the ever-present danger of enemies like her malicious brother. She admired it and dripped some sand as garnish. Then she set about decorating it with the seashells she'd collected. Although she had a desire to doll it up with pretty things like shells and starfish, she was by no means a typical girl. She liked boy things like cars and motorcycles and had forsaken frilly dolls from an early age.

The little girl looked over at her mother, reclining on a beach chair, shades on, suit bone-dry. She'd decided she'd be prettier than her mother—as pretty as her mother had always wanted to be. That's why her mother didn't like her, she reasoned with a precocious shrug. But it didn't bother her, for she was Daddy's favorite and he would always look after her. He was at the snack stand getting hot dogs and Cokes, but he would return soon and they would all have lunch.

This was the Macchiato family as it stood then. Daddy Macchiato—Arnoldo to his boss, Arnie to friends—was a moderately successful insurance salesman. His parents had been born in Calabria, but they'd left Italy in the thirties, during Mussolini's reign. Arnie, born in Hoboken, had married a Presbyterian girl, a sin which his family had never forgiven. But she was a good wife and a good enough mother, and he respected her. She'd arrived as a temp at his insurance office one day and came back a week later as his wife. They'd bought a fine, comfortable house in Lawrence,

Long Island. The price was high for their means but the neighborhood was secure and property values were always climbing. They were happy, now happier with two kids, and Arnie thanked God dutifully every night for his good fortune.

The little girl ran to help him carry the hot dogs the last twenty feet. He hollered and guffawed and put the food down on the hot sand so that he could swing his sweetheart over his head. She purred with pleasure. The little girl identified with her father so much that years later she would do what he'd done: she would marry a Presbyterian—but a far greater catch—for she would marry Kirk Carver, king of the BMW dealerships, a rich man by her father's standards and probably by most people's. In doing so, her name would change from Patricia Macchiato to Patricia Carver, and only the relatives would know she was Catholic, for she had light skin and dirty-blond hair on account of her mother.

It was to this skin that Mrs. Macchiato applied Coppertone suntan lotion on that Memorial Day. Patricia patiently allowed her to apply it; she knew it would prevent the burns which she hated even more than a beachless day. After submitting to the cold, creamy lotion, she ran back to her castle. It was under siege. A young boy, not her brother, was peeling away the shells and destroying the tunnels. Patricia ran to the rescue, and threw sand at the young boy, who then fled, only to come back a moment later offering a new shell as reparation. Patricia, struck immediately by his gentlemanly quality, accepted the gift and asked the boy his name. *Tony*, he replied. He'd gone by Tony since he could remember, and though only nine now, he knew he would always be called Tony.

Tony, she repeated to herself. She liked the name and said so, and the little boy was pleased. For although he didn't know much about girls and was suspicious of them as any self-respecting boy his age would be, he thought the girl perhaps the prettiest he had ever seen. Though too thin, she had brown eyes of magnificent luster and a creamy complexion that complemented her beautiful braids. She would be a ravishing woman, all aunts and uncles fore-casted—and it was true, for she would be sought after by many and courted by the town. Eventually she would fall for a man of riches, for that had always drawn her. For now, she thanked Tony, the shell-giver, and forgave him his mischief. Tony went back to his family's umbrella, but he would never be the same.

At home in Glen River that night, Tony said his prayers. He first prayed for his mother who was ill at the time. Then he prayed that the girl he'd seen on the beach that day would once again appear to him, either in real life or in his dreams. His wishes would be answered, and doubly so, for she would appear in both places. But for reality he would have to wait awhile. He knew instinctively that he would. For even at that age he knew that beautiful girls are hard to find and that the most beautiful often remain aloof, especially from less beautiful boys.

Tony's mother died three months later. Her lung cancer had metastasized and she'd refused chemotherapy. The past weeks had been a time of merely waiting. The trip to the beach was one of his father's rare kindnesses, inspired by his wife's wish to see the seashore one last time. Immediately after her death, he started the drinking that would never leave him. To Tony it was almost a relief for, contrary to the case with many drunks, his cruelty was blunted by the spiraling torpor of gin and whiskey.

Tony never really grieved for his mother. Instead, over the next two years he chose to grieve for a girl he didn't know. He blotted out his mother's image from dreams, waking hours, even the walls of his room—he replaced it with the silhouette of a pixie, a skinny beachcomber with cream-colored skin and nice eyes. This pixie he searched for in shopping malls and on street corners, in video arcades and movie theaters. He never doubted that one day he would see her, but he wondered why God was taking his time to deliver the wish that, after all, he'd applied for so long ago. He often begged his father to take him to the beach—to see the seashore, he said. But the father was finished taking people to see the seashore. It killed them in the end, he'd decided.

3

He counted through the small window: seven paces to the left and then six to the right; then again, seven to the left and six to the right—the lack of symmetry bothered him. He would've figured a lawyer to pace evenly, or at least pretend to. He shared the same suspicion of lawyers that most people did. And this lawyer he was more than suspicious of. Maybe because he was paranoid anyway. Maybe because the Court had appointed him. Maybe because he wore ugly loafers that didn't match his suit—a suit that didn't connote success, with its poor tailoring and need of pressing.

He'd waltzed into the secure conference room with a smile and a handshake. Alan Strasser, he'd explained, an attorney from the public defender's office. Tony McMahon couldn't have been less interested. He knew what the lawyer wanted. He knew what a game it would be. It occurred to him as pathetic that although this man was the only advocate he had in the entire world, he immediately detested him. Although he knew Strasser meant as well for him as anyone could, he knew that what he himself wanted was so much more complex than what anyone could argue for in his behalf—or even wish upon him. Of course, he wanted to get out of jail and be acquitted of this crime, but beyond that his only wishes were fantasies which were void of writs, motions, procedures, rulings and verdicts.

Strasser placed a file on the table.

"Mr. McMahon. I'm not sure if you heard what I said. I'm an attorney from the public defender's office. I've been appointed to represent you at your arraignment." This time Strasser sat down in the high-backed wooden chair directly across from his client.

"I heard you, Mr. Strasser." Tony knew this was to be a storytelling session but he didn't feel like narrating.

"If you don't want me to represent you, you're welcome to choose someone else, but I come free, and from what I hear that's about all you can afford." He waited a suitable pause. "Good. Now what you're going to have to do today is tell me everything, right from the beginning. I'm working on getting them to set bail for you, but that's going to be tough since they think you're a big risk not to appear—I see you've got a prior arrest record—and this was a heck of a crime." He looked up at Tony. "Not that I definitely won't get you out of this, but it's going to be tough, like I said.

"Now let's just start from the beginning. Tell me what

happened. Don't leave a thing out. Believe me, I've heard it all."

Tony knew instinctively that Strasser was a poor practitioner, scared of the courtroom and inept at the law. It mattered little, though. He wouldn't be making any deals and he knew that's all Strasser had come to do.

"There's nothing to say except that I was driving along in my rebuilt Mustang when the cops pulled me over and arrested me." Tony knew that the court-appointed public defender had grown apprehensive that he was one of those rare defendants who insists on innocence and refuses to cop a plea.

"Look, Tony—if I can call you Tony." He raised his eyebrows in deference. "You're going to have to be straight with me and tell me everything. This prosecutor's got a heck of a good case against you—like I say—a letter to your loved one threatening to blow her away. So you're hung, OK. But this prosecutor, he's so scared he doesn't know what to do. He's a young guy. He doesn't want to take this to trial. He can't fight. He probably doesn't know what a courtroom looks like," Strasser laughed thinly. "He wants an easy score. You can give it to him and save yourself. Just plead to a lesser charge. That's all this guy wants. I've been up against him a hundred times."

"If the guy can't fight, then why wouldn't we want to go to court?"

Strasser hadn't even seen that question coming. Tony felt sorry for him. He could picture him during cross-examination: sweating, quivering, mopping his brow and cursing at the judge. They had sent Tony a gutter attorney with scuffed loafers. That's how much they respected him—these courts that would decide his fate. He smiled despite himself.

"What are you smiling at? Believe me you've got no reason to be smiling. We can't fight this guy because his case is too good, like I say. He's got the letters and believe me he'll have more—lab stuff, ballistics probably. You're hung. But I can cut the rope and have you in prison for a while. You'll get out on good behavior. You're a nice guy. Any parole board can see that. We'll get the charge way down. You'll plead to second degree, we'll work that out. They'll buy second degree. We'll at least get that."

"Do you think I did it?"

Strasser looked at him directly. "Yes."

"Why?"

"I know a couple of their cards. There'll be more dealt at arraignment—but we'll start with this. They found an unmailed letter you wrote your dead girlfriend saying how much you couldn't wait to see her dead. In it, you cleverly mention wanting to kill her husband too. More than that I don't know. But who needs a jury. That's motive, means, everything. But if you want to really do this, we'll do this. Let me take notes."

Strasser pulled a legal pad from his briefcase, along

with a ballpoint pen. He looked at Tony quizzically, with an odd mixture of cynicism and interest that he reserved for people who truly puzzled him. "OK. Let's go by the book then and see what we have here. Now where were you between eleven and two on the night of March 16?"

"On my way home from work."

"Where's work?"

"The Anchor 'n Sail restaurant—across from the train tracks in Syosset."

"OK, fine. What time did you leave?"

"Around eleven-thirty."

"Not a bad start. OK and you got home when, just before midnight?"

"No, around three-thirty."

"Why?"

"I got a flat."

Strasser threw up his hands. "Come on, you shmuck, don't waste my time."

"Look, I can't help it if I got a flat," said Tony, crossing his legs and lighting a cigarette from Strasser's pack.

"Did you call a tow truck? Did someone come by who would've seen you around that time?"

"No. I changed it myself."

Strasser turned red, but he held his lip steady and leaned across the table. "Was there not a soul on the whole Island that saw you that night after you left work?"

"May, the waitress at the coffee shop, saw me."

"What time was that?"

"Three."

Strasser put his pad away. He hadn't taken down a word. "You're hung. We did it by the book and you're more hung than ever. You better make a deal and fast."

"Maybe I will."

"Good. I'll handle your arraignment Wednesday and I'll meet with the prosecutor that afternoon. I can guarantee you second degree. Like I say, he doesn't want to fight." Strasser took back his cigarettes, dropped them in the briefcase and snapped it shut. He rang for the guard. "You've come to your senses." Strasser turned to walk out.

"Strasser," Tony stopped him.

"Yes?" he asked turning.

"I don't want to rot away here."

"So what do you want to do about it?"

Tony wasn't averse to dealmaking on principle. But he had a different conception of that kind of thing than Strasser. He knew Strasser was so scared that he'd get himself transferred if the case went past the grand jury. Yet, he sensed he didn't need Strasser anyway. He had faith in his own ability to bend destiny, to make deals, to go free.

"I'll make a deal."

"Good. I'll get the paperwork done."

"There's no paperwork needed. Leave your briefcase at home."

In his mind's prison meanderings, among the cold steel and the pale white light of the cellblock, within himself and without the world, Tony was certain of one truth: When you make a deal with the devil, the only currency you need is your soul.

4

After several years of commuting, the Macchiato family decided that Lawrence, a South Shore community, was too far from Arnie's Hicksville offices. They contacted some realtors, put their house on the market, and went hunting on the North Shore. After looking in six or seven areas, they found a nice three-bedroom in a sleepy suburban community that was only ten minutes from the office. They broke in the new house in late summer, having timed the move to coincide with the beginning of the school year. Their new address was a grand one, thought Mrs. Macchiato: 11 Bancroft Circle, Glen River, Long Island. It bespoke elegance and prosperity.

But twelve-year-old Patricia was annoyed at her mother's excitement. It had become clear to her that they weren't rich. There had been some kids at St. Anne's, her old parochial school, that had lawyer and doctor parents who drove Cadillacs and Mercedes. They'd lived in more fashionable neighborhoods, with wider streets and the houses farther apart. She'd seen one of these "rich" homes once— a magnificent glassed-in triple decker, with a tennis court and a pool. She'd immediately grown ashamed of her family's old humble home—suddenly scornful of the garbage disposal she'd once been so proud of; embarrassed by her erstwhile favorite couch in the living room which now seemed worn; mortified by the small yard she'd always found a magical playland. The move didn't help any, for the new house she found even more distasteful and disgustingly common with its prefab style and aluminum siding. To see her mother croon and beam at her new stationery with the new "chic" address was almost too much for young Patricia to bear. She even started to resent the presence of her father, whom she blamed for their not being wealthy. Right before school was ready to start up that week, Patricia considered running away.

But the thought of being poor and without a bed scared her even more than the thought of being middle-class and without a maid. So she endured and started classes with her older brother at the Glen River Middle School that September. She was at least happy not to be in Catholic school anymore, with the miserable sisters and the snooty girls. Though she considered public school beneath her, she knew instinctively that there she'd be one of the wealthier students.

○ ◐ ○

Tony McMahon was counting his pencils. He'd always been a very methodical and conscientious youngster, and counting the pencils was a necessary prelude to the school day. He had four, which would be enough even if he had to give two to Cody, the ninth grader on his bus who bullied him. He packed his knapsack extra carefully, for this was no ordinary day. It was the first day of classes, but more importantly, his first day in the Glen River Middle School as a seventh grader. He'd been bumped ahead an extra grade because of his excellent test scores. His father had opposed the move, telling the teacher he didn't want any "uppity" sons—but the teacher, as good ones can, knew which of the two McMahons was the wiser, and she sent the younger across to the other building with big, thick seventh-grade books and good wishes.

So Tony was sure to get things right. He didn't want to please his father by failing on the first day. Four pencils, four notebooks, an extra eraser, a candy bar (for a snack, bribe, barter—whatever need presented itself), his gym clothes, and a three-ring binder all went into the knapsack. He was proud of the tidy package as he zippered it all up and went outside to wait for the bus.

The bus ride was always his favorite part, as long as Cody was playing hooky—which was often. No Cody. He smiled to himself as he took his seat. That meant he had all four pencils and the candy bar all the way through the day. He opened his bag to gloat over the contents once again and double-check the numbers. He counted it all out. Soon tiring of that, he watched the view—rows of well-appointed, orderly homes—passing by on his left. The bus stopped at a particularly clean and white one. He noticed that this house hadn't been a stop last year. He eagerly looked out the window. New kids were always good news: they usually took the brunt of the bus-ride bullying.

What he saw caused his open bag to spill off his lap and under the seat behind him, his well-counted pencils to roll to the back of the bus, and his immaculate notebooks to tarnish themselves on the gritty floor. For what he saw couldn't have been real. It was an image from unsteady dreams and fantasies, something he associated with summer, shells and freedom. He saw his skinny beachcomber. Her face was unmistakable. The hair was longer and luxurious, but she still had the same creamy skin, combined with those very fetching eyes.

She came on with an older boy. They wended their way to the back of the bus, unsure about where they should sit—which of course they would be, for that was a ritualistic knowledge, governed by complex rules of behavior that took at least three or four grades' worth of bus rides to learn. Everyone silently stared, which was as much a part of the initiation as anything else. She handled it well, thought Tony: Without returning so much as a single glare, she chose the very last seat, confidently occupied the one across from it with her book bag, and motioned for the boy to sit in front of her. Tony was impressed by this settlement of three seats, where most kids would have claimed one. It spoke of confidence and a mercenary sense of entitlement, qualities which would always capture him.

He turned back to the front and concentrated on getting together his belongings. Everything except the pencils he quickly recovered. He knew these would never be seen again, for most had probably been scavenged. The ones that hadn't had probably come to a rest at the foot of his beachcomber. Retrieving them was out of the question.

But suddenly his precise and fastidious spirit had been damaged. He no longer cared if he had those four pencils, let alone whether his notebooks were spotted with sneaker prints. He didn't even care whether he had a dollar to buy new ones at the school store. At that point he might as well have left the knapsack behind altogether. For that day marked the end of Tony as a student of any school subjects. He would from now on be a student only of his beachcomber: taking extensive notes on her movements, calculating her moods, memorizing her outfits, reciting her name, writing compositions about her eyes and book reports about her skin. For on that day, two years and 105 days after he'd first offered a shell to a pretty little girl, Tony was eternally damned.

5

In America, mail order is king.

Tony Grasso McMahon knew that better than anyone. From now on he figured to be living his life through it. To that end, he'd started to send away for everything—from mouthwash to college degrees. Nearly all of his requests were denied shipment by the prison warden, but not his latest. For as of last Tuesday, Tony had enrolled in a correspondence course to become a minister. He would soon join the ranks of the mail-order clergy.

He'd seen the small ad in one of the few periodicals he was allowed to borrow from the prison library, an ecumenical religious weekly. The promise of full minister certification was made in exchange for twelve dollars and the completion of a few forms. Even as correspondence courses go, it looked to be far from rigorous. There was no guarantee of a congregation or a job, or even a church to accept him, with or without a flock. Yet, the application looked easy enough and promised instant entry into a profession Tony had once considered.

The enrollment form had asked several pointed questions, all of which he answered truthfully and concisely:

(1) **Have you always had faith in a divine presence?**
Yes.

(2) **Have you ever been ordained as a priest, minister, rabbi, etc. previously?**
No.

(3) **Do you feel equipped to handle a life of sacrifice and toil for the sake of humankind?**
Yes.

(4) **Do you believe that humankind's salvation must come in the form of religious faith?**
Sort of.

(5) **Can you furnish a reference upon request?**
Yes.

(6) **How did you hear of The Church of Community Faith's ministry program?**
From an ad in <u>Common Healing Magazine.</u>

(7) **Have you ever engaged in a homosexual act?**
No.

(8) **Have you ever been convicted of a felony?**
No.

Tony mailed in the form to the Tallahassee offices of the Church of Community Faith with a short note politely asking them to bill his father for the twelve-dollar fee. After that there was nothing left to do except wait for his shiny document of Ministerial certification to come in the mail. He assigned a place for it on the wall in his cell, next to the makeshift bookshelf with the Bible and his magazines.

His father had forbidden the seminary, insisting his son wouldn't be as "poor as some leper priest" but rather, a moneymaker, an earner—someone to support his old man when his old man would be too drunk to drive to work. As it turned out, Tony had eventually decided that his priestly ambitions were in conflict with his desire to wed Patricia. So he'd forsaken his calling as God had Jesus on the cross.

Now that Patricia was dead, he felt the closest he could come to her was through religion. Faith, if it was worth anything at all, could reunite them. He hoped his minister's certificate would arrive before his arraignment, which had been scheduled for next week. It would be nice, while standing before the judge, awaiting the formal charges, to be able to make his plea with the knowledge that he was a man of the cloth.

These days, a priest seems to fall from grace at least every other Sunday. And when it happens, even good Catholics nudge one another over the paper and say, *I told you so. He always did seem strange.* But that wasn't the way it was years ago. Religion used to be powerful. When Tony McMahon was growing up, religion was the only power besides money, which remained powerful, and country, which went the way of God.

As a young choir boy, he'd been seduced by the smell of incense and the bold sermons that Father Marsiglia relied on—that his father, that his mother, that everyone relied on—to get through to the next week. Sermons, preaching, words—the Word.

Tony had, in fact, always wanted to be something, at least on the surface anyway, unlinked to religion—like a rock star. Tone-deaf from an early age, however, he'd decided to curtail those ambitions. Not that such a disability in itself would have been a hindrance. As his father used to joke, it probably would have served to advance his career. But Tony didn't like the idea of struggle. He preferred to find something which suited him well enough, so that he could wear his chosen vocation like a dapper, well-tailored suit over the talents of his form, without any alterations needed.

He reasoned that the worship of a host of parishioners was the closest he would ever come to the adulation of a fluttering of rock groupies. The roles of clergyman and rock star—so patently different in their philosophical sources—seemed to Tony more linked than distant, more connected by motives of megalomania and neediness than separated by the cross-purposes often ascribed them.

Besides, religion was about sainthood. And from the earliest age, Tony knew he was a saint. He always stopped to help blind people cross the street, always dropped a dime in the beggar's cup, always participated in the March of Dimes walkathon. In the mirror—even as a child—he saw taut, austere features: thin hungry lips, a stooped, gaunt frame, burdened eyebrows, a nub of a chin. These, he assumed, were all characteristics of a saint. It didn't deter him that he wasn't attractive. Plainness was surely an asset to the hopelessly charitable. Through it, he could relate to the human condition. And through that, he could practice the essence of martyrdom: gut-wrenching self-pity.

That night, as had become his recent custom, he read a passage of the Bible before going to bed. It was one of his favorites—one his Aunt Tia had always read to him—provided that his father was too busy watching football to notice—when he'd go to her house for Thanksgiving supper after his mother had died. Aunt Tia had liked to read him New Testament scripture, but Tony had preferred the stories of the Old Testament. She indulged her young nephew's wishes, always sure to remind him that the Old Testament was a "violent, Hebrew book" not to be read too often. But she would always begin, as he did now, by making the sign of the cross across her chest.

It was the story of Abraham and Isaac. To Tony, this story of a father commanded to kill his son was the essence of faith, loyalty, sacrifice and love. Yet he never finished reading the verses, for soon his imagination would take over. He pictured himself as Abraham, holding the knife aloft above his son's tired, bare body. He pictured the terror of Isaac, the eyelids pasted back with fear, the legs and arms quivering with their anticipation of the fall of the blade.

But in this imagined scene, the intervening voice of God would never come. And the blade would drop unfettered. And the screams would pierce the heavens. And the blood would flow onto the grasses. For God did not always test faith without high stakes. Sometimes sacrifice meant sacrifice—not a false alarm. In his daydream, he would pick up the dying Isaac and hold him up to God and moan:

This is the child I have slaughtered for you, the blood of my blood, the love of my love. Why lord did you allow me to complete this deed?

And God would respond:

Your loved ones you shall offer unto me. For here with me they shall always serve you, and be loyal unto you, While on the planet of man they shall wander into the arms of the devil and shall sin.

And Tony knew God was right. Because loved ones just plain couldn't be trusted on earth. Too many temptations. Sometimes it was better to hand them up to heaven for safekeeping.

6

Worship comes in many forms. But it's a tricky business—sometimes even beyond the grasp of everything except absolute faith. For idols can be smashed, scripture burned, mantras forgotten, temples forsaken. Even faith can be stood on its head. And faith in a woman, that's a whole other story. Or so thought Tony on a fateful autumn day.

On that first day of school he'd checked on the seventh-grade list and discovered her name, Patricia Macchiato of 11 Bancroft Circle, Glen River, 883–7897. Now that he had words to attach to the face, he repeated them to himself relentlessly, mumbling the syllables under his breath. He thought the name beautiful, strong, lyrical, and perfectly suited to a girl like her. He'd taken to writing her name during class on his notebooks, starting in the upper-left-hand corner, as if beginning a composition, and working his way down in a looping pattern that left his hand contorted and sweaty.

To Tony's delight, Patricia Macchiato had been assigned to three out of his five classes. Not that he'd taken advantage of such proximity to talk to her. He was certain she wouldn't remember him from the beach, and he would've been far too terrified to approach her anyway. His main contact consisted of sitting diagonally behind her in social studies. This allowed a unique angle from which to view her abundant hair, highlighted auburn from the summer months. It wasn't exactly an artist's perspective, but it did allow him to gorge on her locks unobserved.

Tony developed a logbook of her features, both the assets and the deficiencies. He divided the page in half lengthwise with a red line, as in a stenographic pad, and wrote the headings at the top in his schoolboy scrawl: *Good Things About Patricia Macchiato* on the left, *Bad Things About Patricia Macchiato* on the right. He added entries to the left column daily, as he noticed items that couldn't go unmentioned—like the way she flipped her hair before answering a question in class, or her small ears, or the industrial-looking rainboots that only a boy would don, or the habit of stifling a yawn in class by rubbing her wrist across her nose, or her dislike of hamsters that she announced in science class one day (Tony cast his hamster out into the Glen River streets that night), or the way she took notes so that her elbow ended up pointing at the teacher, or her weird half-smile that she'd never yet bestowed upon him, or her knobby knees, or her barely perceptible sigh when she was bored, or even her unforgiving eyes. These were all meticulously entered in his log with the date on which they were first noted. For example, *neat boots, blue, kind boys wear*—Oct. 3.

After a month of compulsive recording, he realized that most of the entries were not really physical items or features but rather idiosyncratic mannerisms. This pleased him, for in his precociousness he reasoned that his devotion to Patricia must be more sophisticated if based on such things. He imagined penning her a long epistle enumerating all such abstract traits of her being. He even started to compose such a letter one day, but his will broke thin and he flushed it down the toilet.

He noticed something else about his logbook—that he'd not yet made a single entry in the right column. He rejoiced in this as an unmistakable sign of Patricia's perfection. He even toyed with the idea of ripping out the right half in arrogant certainty that she could never disappoint him. But in the end he decided against it. Women, he knew, were mercurial. Better to leave open the possibility for fault. He even began to look forward to recording one defect, so that he could note its frivolity, and smile. He imagined himself entering something like *chooses red M&M's over yellow* and laughing at this deviation from perfection. To him it was a grave taboo to make such a choice, of course. But in a pretty girl it seemed somehow a mild infraction— a mere foible.

So the right column remained blissfully blank all through

October. It was a beautiful month in Glen River, with the trees hunching in their autumn bloom and pumpkins popping up on stoops and in windowsills. The football team was practicing everyday on the South Field of the high school and the chill gave way to a two-week balm of Indian summer.

The middle schoolers had to wander by the South Field to catch their buses, and many of them would dawdle to catch glimpses of the Glen River Red Devils, the pride and joy of the school. Football, hockey and lacrosse were the sports worthy of hero-making on Long Island. All seventh-grade boys wanted to be future varsity quarterbacks and all seventh-grade girls wanted to be their future dates. It was a rare student who wasn't somewhat awed by the spectacle of grunting, hitting, blocking, and tackling on an autumn afternoon.

It was Tony's habit to follow Patricia out of English, the last-period class which they conveniently shared, and watch her amble to her locker, chat with the two or three of her new female friends, and collect her books for the trip home. He'd follow her out into the courtyard, over the chain-link fence and across to the high-school campus. It was considered dangerous for a boy to make this particular journey—to traverse the high-school parking lot and follow it around to the South Field and the bus loading zone—because ninth and tenth graders didn't take kindly to middle-school boys coming across. So most boys walked the whole perimeter to avoid trouble. For a girl it was dangerous, but in different ways. Some went across for the thrill of seeing what would happen. It was rare that anything actually did.

Patricia went every day and Tony followed her. He was too concerned with not being noticed by her to worry about being bloodied or bruised by high schoolers. He would hide behind the bleachers as Patricia stopped to watch the football practices. He wondered what she could find so interesting in such a brutish, boring game—one which he despised privately, because he never could admit that to his classmates.

One day a group of players pausing to take their water break at the sideline decided to engage the pretty fan in conversation. She looked tall and mature for her age, especially the way she wore her hair now: long, in a straight sheen, with no sign of the abandoned stages of pigtails, braids and curls. Tony thought nothing of this at first. He often noticed groups of girls talking to the players and assumed that they were as if two different species—older varsity men and sweet prim girls. Never did it occur to him, perhaps because he'd not yet taken biology, that there is one rule which evolution defined long ago: young females like older males, and vice versa. But to the fledgling Tony, this mating ritual on the football field appeared as cross-speciation does to a zoologist: a physiological improbability.

The socializing between Patricia and the football players started to become such a common occurrence that Tony grew tired of waiting behind the bleachers. He would fidget and then finally sit on the grass to linger until his beachcomber would proceed to their bus. Once there, he was calm: He could watch her unobstructed from roughly the same angle he'd surveyed her in social studies class.

One day, after the accustomed minutes of laughing and talking, the football players retreated to their practice as they usually did, waving good-bye to Patricia and running to make the coach's whistle. But Patricia didn't leave. Instead, she dropped her book bag to the ground, sat on top of it and watched. Tony had no idea what this meant. He did know that the bus would leave in about three minutes—they always cut it close anyway—and that they were bound to miss it unless she hurried along. He paced in an agonized way behind the bleachers like a boy desperate to go to the bathroom, willing her to get up and walk to the buses. But she remained where she was, her hair wisping in the breezes, her arms crossed languidly in her skirted lap.

Panic-stricken, he looked at his watch. It was three-thirty-nine. By now the bus surely would have left. He strained to see if he could refract the yellow blur that was the bus in the parking lot, but there was nothing. The afternoon grew chilly. Patricia put on her jean jacket while Tony resigned himself to a long wait on the wet grass beneath the bleachers.

Finally, an hour later, the whistle blew and the players went in to change. Patricia got up to leave and Tony was delighted. He realized that she would have to walk the two miles home, an exertion that would allow him to follow in contented silence watching the sway of her book bag and the patter of her feet. This was a bargain he hadn't counted on. He was suddenly grateful to God for having instructed her to wait out the entire practice and ignore the yellow bus. Of course it was silly that they should take the bus every day when the quiet blocks of Glen River afforded far greater intimacy for his worship.

He followed her excitedly around to Broom Hill Road, the street which bordered the school and would eventually lead them to Bancroft Circle. But Patricia stopped at the corner and Tony stopped twenty paces behind her. He was puzzled. Had she lost her way? Could it be that she didn't really know the route home? This possibility excited him further for he felt he might get up the nerve to ask her if she needed help in navigating. Just then an old Volkswagen sped around the corner and screeched to a stop. The door opened, an older boy stepped out, allowed Patricia to get in, and followed her, closing the door behind them. The car took off with another manic burst and Tony watched them cruise down Broom Hill.

It dawned on him only a full minute later that he was completely alone. The field was empty, the bus lot windswept, the streets still. There were no voices or laughter. Dusk was falling fast. An empty school is a sad thing.

Before going to bed that night he brushed his teeth, got out his clothes for the next day, and took out his logbook, for it was time to make a new entry. He flattened down the binding and scripted in a painfully neat hand, the neatest he could muster, in the right column:

can't be trusted

He wrote it in pencil—with hopes that it could be erased eventually. But even then he suspected it might as well have been etched in the most indelible of inks.

7

Day thirty-three was without water. Due to a defect in the prison plumbing, the pipes had been dry since late the night before. Security had been increased to offset a riot. And it wasn't hard to see how such a thing might happen with the toilets not flushing and the faucets merely buckling and groaning under the turn of the spigot.

To Tony, it was a complete calamity. Not because his arraignment was to take place that day and he wouldn't be able to shave. He discounted that as meaningless. But the greatest pleasures of servitude were his daily libations, which he would take with astonishing ritual, to a rhythm that punctuated his days as steadily as the wake-up bells and body counts.

Water, he realized, was his most loyal jail companion. He flushed with it, shaved with it, touched it to his face and lips to wake up. On water he depended for cleanliness, which had become a savage fetish. He washed his hands, by his last count, an average of twenty times a day; wet his hair ten times; scrubbed under his fingernails five. If a section of dust appeared in the cell corner, he would attack it with savage impatience, dampening the cloth he reserved for such purposes and swabbing it down. No dust particle was too small to avoid his scrutiny. Several times a day he would incline his head at different angles to catch the ones that had hidden in shadows. He was sane enough to find his own behavior odd, but he knew it was a symptom of confinement, of having so small an environment that he needed to protect it.

Standing in the center of it, he remembered that Strasser was due to collect him with the guards at noon and escort him to court. He had decided upon his plea with very little effort. He looked forward to a vindication at trial, but dreaded a protracted and sensationalistic one, with his name figuring prominently in the papers. He knew his case had already started to attract more and more media attention. Like a sleeper movie that shocks the critics and delights the studios, the Carver killings had begun to pull in big receipts. Now that the case appeared to involve a love triangle, and Long Island mayhem had slowed to a trickle, reporters had perked up to its new promise.

Today he would declare his innocence to the court. He turned to look at his ministry certificate which clung less than handsomely on the wall. He hadn't been allowed to frame it. As a result, he'd had to tape it up, but he was quite proud of it all the same. And today, as a registered minister, he would declare his innocence to the court.

Tony had decided to get rid of Strasser right after the arraignment. He'd known he would have to do it before the pretrial motions began. And he'd come to see it as an act of mercy both to himself and to Strasser. He'd already retained the services of a trial lawyer noted for his dramatics. He'd written to several lawyers, asking them to take his case pro bono. His inquiry had fallen flat until a big feature appeared in one of the dailies. After that, many a lawyer had written him.

He'd decided on Ralph Barolo, a Long Island native with a thick accent and an expensive Rolex on his wrist. These two details, Tony immediately decided, were the signals of success. Besides, Barolo had promised to win the case, and that was more than anyone else had promised. His father would have said that such arrogance was the sign of a real con artist. But Tony had learned that raw arrogance, utterly void of apology or discomfiture—the type that's so unforgiving of itself that it becomes seductive—is what rules the world.

Barolo hadn't been interested in guilt or innocence. Not once had he asked whether Tony had done anything wrong. Instead, he asked pointed questions about the night of the killings. Unlike Strasser, he saw Tony's lack of an alibi as a strength. What jury, he asked with a hefty laugh, would believe that Tony wouldn't have made sure to have had someone see him before three in the morning if he'd committed a crime around midnight? In this age of killers being savvy to alibis, even falsifying them with dash and ingenuity by means of answering-machine messages and altered faxes, who would believe that this smart, well-spoken kid, a promising student at a community college, wouldn't have done the same?

When Tony admitted that his letter to Patricia had indeed spoken of death in intimate detail, Barolo waxed philosophical. Of course, death and passion were interlinked, but letters were poetry. And poetry, he could convince a jury, was the signpost of a man with sensitivity—one working through horrible desires, not acting upon them.

Barolo was fanatically excited about Tony's case, hailing it as remarkable that it had even gotten past the grand jury, so circumstantial was it. Shaking his fist in the meeting room, he declaimed against juries that could try men on the basis of a letter. What kind of a country were we living in that allowed such things to happen? He banged his Rolexed wrist on the table. *A police state,* he screamed!

This Barolo, whom Tony had dubbed the Dictator for his gesticulating and his stocky physique, could rant and rave, cursing for hours against all manner of injustice. With a fanatical grin, he could dismiss fanatical prosecutors. With a tyrannical grunt, he could condemn tyrannical courts. With a totalitarian wave, he could avenge totalitarian laws. Tony knew that if anyone could buy his freedom, Barolo, with all his obscenity and braggadocio, was the one.

Tony had worried about not remembering the content of the letter, and Barolo had assured him that they would know everything following discovery. Barolo had dismissed this concern, ridiculing instead the idea of charging Tony with murder when one of the victims was found clutching a revolver. Tony had complained that the maid, and perhaps the children, had often seen him spying on the house. Barolo had parried that any jury would be sympathetic to his plight. Instead of refuting the frequency of visits to the Carver house, he would play up that point and emphasize the malignant seed such uninvited visits might have planted in the mind of a paranoid Kirk Carver.

To Barolo, it was so simple. Kirk Carver, upon discovering his young wife was being routinely followed by a younger man, grew insanely and wrongly suspicious. He snapped, and slaughtered his family, then himself. Tony considered this. He'd seen photos of Carver and had come to know him through the newspapers. And though Tony had certainly hated him, he'd never considered Kirk Carver capable of such a deed as murder. Instead, he'd thought him to be a devoted family man—perhaps meekly dominated by his assertive wife. Yet, many men of supposedly stellar reputation had cracked throughout history. That was the bloom of tragedy. It would be nothing new.

Then the water sputtered on, for he'd left the tap open. Tony took some of its coolness and pasted back his bangs. Then he lathered and washed his face. With cheeks still wet, he looked into the makeshift mirror he'd fashioned from a piece of plastic wrap stretched to a taut finish over a square of black cardboard. The shadowy, hardly discernible form that was his face loomed there unsmilingly. It wasn't a clear looking-glass, but he was happy for that.

Not that it was a hideous face. It was almost pleasant, with strong features—somewhat pockmarked, though that only showed under a real mirror. Yet, it wasn't a dependable face, he knew.

And try as they might, juries had a hard time looking past such things as a defendant's smile or lack of one, his stooped or straight back, his small or large nose, his gnarled or even hands, his solid or wheezy voice. Juries were as unscientific as the rest of us, as much guided by prejudice, personalities, pretense, persuasion and passions as the souls they were called upon to judge.

He looked at himself in the homemade mirror and saw ambiguous features, a liability as a suspect. For on a sunny day, to a kind grandmotherly pensioner, whose husband's angioplasty had just been successful, his was the face of a decent person. But to a sadistic schoolteacher in September, whose application for a mortgage had just been denied by the bank, his was the face of a killer.

8

To most, it was puppy love. But to Tony, it was viper venom—black, viscous, seething, and without antidote:

His beachcomber had a boyfriend.

Thomas R. Cuccio, dubbed Koosh by his friends, was a junior, a star linebacker and running back, charismatic, leader of *the* group at school, none too bright, exceedingly handsome and, as of Halloween night, Patricia Macchiato's sole reason for being.

Though she was in seventh and he in eleventh grade, an unaccustomed age-spread by anyone's standards, the two had taken to each other without a hitch. His friends had teased him at first, admonishing him not to "hurt" her and calling him a child molester. But it was clearly sour grapes. For Patricia Macchiato, though only just thirteen, could have passed for three years older and would have been one of the most desirable girls in school no matter what her birth date. She grew more beautiful by the day, especially as more and more attention was lavished upon her. Her clothes were sophisticated, her manner mature, her lips sensual. She was more stylish than many of the older girls and thus in the eyes of all, more attractive.

The older girls hated her instantly. From the moment she'd started ogling football players, with her not-so-shy smile and skimpy outfits, she'd been singled out as a major threat. Now that she was dating Koosh, one of the most desirable boys on campus, she'd been blacklisted to an extent that made any socializing with her own sex impossible. But that could not have concerned her. She'd set out not to make friends with girls but to capture the attention of boys. And that she'd done with an alacrity even the boys found alarming.

She jealously guarded every moment with Koosh. She snuck over to the high-school campus whenever she had a free period and sat with him in the cafeteria. Patricia would stare at her broad-shouldered linebacker and think with joy of his glowing popularity, his desirability among all the girls, his command over the boys. For to Patricia, Koosh's currency was solely his status among others. She noticed his fine, dark curls only when she caught another girl staring at them. She considered his charming, friendly manner only when she saw its effect on a teammate. She rhapsodized over his athletic prowess only when she read a worshipful article in the school paper. Without an audience to adore him and hence reflect value unto her, Patricia wouldn't have been the least bit interested.

To Tony, the relationship was a slow death, a miserable

grinding of his emotional clutch. He knew none of the terms of it, had no angle on Patricia's motives, had only known of Koosh in the same way one hears of mythical gods or celebrities. The agony of it wrought his being into a chronic state of dullness.

Upon first learning of their relationship through bathroom gossip and notes graffitied on school desks, he'd disbelieved it. Then he'd noticed Patricia scurrying across the fields to the high school on the heels of classes. He'd witnessed daily what had become the recurring ritual of watching Patricia climb into the car with the football players. Finally, on an unseasonably warm day in late November, he'd spied her sitting on Koosh's lap on the grassy commons in front of the middle school. At that moment, he'd pinched himself viciously with a thumbnail, half to hope it was a nightmare, half to stop himself from crying.

Tony tortured himself endlessly by tracing the movements of the couple as best he could. He was terrified of moments when they might be alone unobserved. He began to reason that what he could see wasn't so bad. But what he couldn't see—his imagination was too vivid to admit to that possibility.

As he'd compulsively listed her traits before, now he logged her movements. At the end of the day he would calculate all the unaccounted-for time, the minutes when she'd escaped his surveillance, and decide that two hours without him couldn't have damaged their own future too much.

He constructed maps of her daily meanderings. A dotted line meant *all alone,* a broad swipe meant *accompanied by Koosh,* a squiggle meant *without apparent destination.* These maps also served to calm him. By tracking her movements he in some sense controlled them.

Valiantly, he tried to sketch her portrait during class, so as to have something that he could frame and put over his desk at home. But his draftsman's abilities were abysmal. The drawings ended up as limp improvisations that served worse than emptiness to evoke her image. No matter how dutifully he tried to capture the hollows of her cheeks, the pout that had become her perpetual classroom expression, or the angles at which she pitched her elbows, he ended up with uncomfortable-looking stick figures that stared back at him with resentment. Had he been schooled in, or at least prone to, discovering abstraction, he could have given expression to his emotions in pencil. But he was not.

He thought of photographing her, but the logistics didn't permit it. Even if he'd had a camera, he wouldn't have had an opportunity to use it. For he couldn't allow her to witness the act, and he had no idea there was such a thing as a telephoto lens. He decided he'd have to wait until the yearbook was published in spring. Then he would cut out her small headshot and mount it on a piece of cardboard. Until then he would have to content himself with his memories, stick figures, and the increasingly shadowy glimpses he was afforded of her during the school day.

As weeks passed he began to move in the complacent haze of one who, recognizing that his rivals and obstacles are infinitely taller than himself, adjusts his yearnings and shrinks them ten sizes. He no longer saw Patricia Macchiato as his potential mate, though he did want to insinuate himself into her life somehow—to find his niche among her grasping psychological needs, to come to be depended on. As a young boy who was unknown to her, he had no idea how to go about this. But he sensed that God would one day present him with the opportunity.

9

He fondled it. What else would you do with a letter that was sealed with a kiss? He followed the outline of each lip, in its pinkish, cheap waxiness and marveled at the way the sight and feel of it affected him. Just the lipstick marks of a woman were enough to excite him after over sixty days in jail. She'd been sure to make the imprints large and suggestive. He imagined the sensuous stamp pads that had done this handiwork and hoped desperately that she'd enclosed a photograph.

It wasn't the first fan letter he'd received. Ever since his name had been published in the paper, the mail had started coming in. At first it was one on Monday, the next on Friday. Lately there'd been at least one every day and by now he had a shoebox-full.

The very first had shocked him. He'd been used to his overwhelmingly predictable mail-call: a legal notice here, a periodical there, a letter from his aunt, an update from his

Ministry, and not much else. Then a letter arrived from a name he didn't know, from a town he'd never visited, let alone could have found on a map. It was a clutching, lonely letter, a work of pure desperation. A widow, lamenting the miserable shadows of her existence, pledged her eternal love for him. She claimed to understand his pain and enclosed her photo. It was a black-and-white glossy, as old and weary as the withered tone of the letter. She labored to express her faith in his innocence and she assured him he would be vindicated at the trial. Tony couldn't understand how she arrived at her decision, but he hoped the jury would use the same calculus. The letter paradoxically irritated him. It seemed in its naiveté to be a dangerous piece of work. What did she know of his guilt or innocence? Like everyone else, she'd never asked. Yet, she'd judged him innocent and now saw him as her salvation. He was repulsed. But not to disappoint her, he scribbled a short response, claiming to be very busy with his legal problems and thanking her for her support.

There'd been other letters, all in the same vein, claiming sympathy for his plight and heralding his innocence as obvious. There'd been some hate mail as well, wishing him a punishment of hellfire and oblivion. These he relished reading and replied to with what he considered very Christian responses, explaining that he, like them, had faith that the Lord would see fit to judge him fairly.

But this newest letter was different. The envelope was of a fine-quality paper, with a sturdy texture that snapped and sprung to life in his hands.

And then there was the kiss.

He opened it slowly, using his fingernail to split the top edge so as not to disturb the seal. The paper, too, was excellent quality, like parchment. It smelled of an exotic perfume. He considered prolonging the pleasure of opening it but then decided he couldn't wait. He sensed there was something too marvelous in its folds. But he was disappointed. The letter was only two pages and lacked a picture.

It was written with lines that were centered strangely and began like so:

It would be hard for me to describe what made me write you, a common prisoner, like this. But just from seeing your photo and reading about you in the paper, I feel I know you so, so well that it can't be an accident. I don't know if you did those sick things people are saying you did. I can tell you that no one here in Garden City could care one way or the other. Here, people want to know about the price of gas and not much else. But I followed your story from the beginning and I get the papers now everyday to try to find something new about you. Please write me and tell me if you killed those people or not. You can tell me the truth. I won't hate you if you did it. But I need your honesty, because I know from your picture you're honest. It's one thing to lie to the police, but it's another to lie to me. I sealed this with a kiss—I think I could love you.

Please write back.

Charlotte Celeste Hinney
Garden City, New York

The sentiment of the letter astonished Tony. It seemed so honest and vulnerable, yet totally accepting. Here was someone who finally asked him if he'd actually done what they said he'd done, expected an honest response and pledged devotion even if he was a murderer. Barolo had forbidden him to respond to any of these letters, but he'd already broken that rule more than once, so he immediately began penning a reply to Charlotte Hinney. He wanted to make it appear as special to her as hers had appeared to him. He took out his notebook and sat on his bed to begin:

Dear Charlotte,

You probably have very little idea how nice it is to get letters in a jail cell. Or maybe you can imagine well enough. What's better than letters are letters from a person who understands you. Your letter was that type. I know we don't know each other. I never did know too many people anyway and I only passed through Garden City once, when I had to pick up some paint cheap.

I don't know anything about you. I don't know what you look like. You I guess from the papers know what I look like though. I was hoping you could put in a photo in your next letter so we can be even. If there's anything I can do for you, let me know. Everyone thinks I'm the one in big trouble which I am. But I still know how to handle a bunch of things. Certainly if you need someone to write to I'm here for that for awhile.

You ask if I did the things they say. You'd be surprised what a strange question that is around here. No one asks you that. They have their own idea about things. The only one who asked me yet besides you was the judge. And still he didn't ask if I did it. He asked if I was guilty. And I'm guilty as hell if you count all the guilt I always feel. But I told him not guilty. I hope that gives you an answer.

Please write soon Charlotte. You can reach me at the same address for awhile. They're not thinking of bail for me anytime soon.

Signed,
Antonio McMahon, Inmate #90245

He folded the letter and began addressing an envelope. Then he sealed the small packet and looked at it disappointedly. It was unimpressive and flimsy—a very short note—but he'd always been too impatient to write long letters. His attention for such things had never been much. Even in prison, with the hours looming before him like a thousand winters, he couldn't get himself to go on to a second page.

He decided to kiss the envelope flap. His was an invisible kiss, a small tender gesture. He considered how a kiss without lipstick was a kiss without a trace. How many kisses did anyone have a trace of? If kisses were like fingerprints, on record with federal agencies, they could be traced. And what if every kiss ever was preserved in such a way with dye or lipstick and dated and filed? You could trace anyone's passions. Tony laughed out loud. It amused him to think of fiancées going to an agency to get a full record of their potential spouse's past loves.

You could spend hours perusing through the stacks of old indiscretions, affairs, jealousies, manipulations, regrets, ecstasies and miseries. One of the last vestiges of privacy would be gone. That, thought Tony, would be a very bad idea. As it is, anyone can ask their lover about what came before them. People do, every day. It's easy to ask the question. But who wants the real answer?

He placed the envelope addressed to Charlotte Celeste Hinney on top of the milk crate that served as a bureau. How strange to get to know someone through the mail. And even stranger was that two things that had always eluded him in real life—a ministership and a woman who could love him—had all of a sudden arrived by first-class post.

10

Warm spring nights were bonfire nights. Anyone who knew anything about Glen River knew that.

As the school year wound down, there were longer and longer days, fewer and fewer feelings of bondage to adults and school, more and more opportunities for Patricia to spend time in the arms of Koosh. The lacrosse team took its spring rites to the field and the cherry blossoms bloomed, classes were held outside, the teachers lost their austere stares. For spring in any school—in any place that observes the ritual by acknowledging that as natural life begins, so should work end—is a time when all rules get broken.

And twelfth graders celebrated their upcoming parole with bonfires on the grounds of abandoned estates. They would pack into cars with kerosene and beer, girls and pot, and head out for the old-money places where the money was so old, even in those years, that it had all but dried up.

It was only a ten-minute drive to nearby Hautucket Bay where old carriage sheds, often so far from the main house as to be worlds unto themselves, afforded the perfect opportunity for playing music and getting high. It was part of the initiation for juniors to scout out the property the night before, choosing places with no security guards or attack dogs. These underage location scouts were held to task for any screwup. They would be beaten later if the police showed up.

Koosh was spared this rite because of his friends in high places. He was elevated to the status of senior and, as such, had the right to invite a girlfriend. There was an undiscussed prohibition on anyone under fifteen being present at these parties. But no one would have dared point that out to Koosh. Some of the older girls prodded their senior boyfriends to make a stir about Patricia's standing invitation, but they were too weak-willed to object and generally too low on the totem of school status to intervene anyway.

Saturday, May 5, was assigned as the night for the first big bonfire. The industrious scouts had scooped a prime spot—a nine-acre estate that was being auctioned for foreclosure in two weeks. There was a barbed-wire fence which was easy to handle, but no alarms, no security and best of all, no residents. There was no furniture either. But that was a minor setback. The rumblings around school got everyone excited. This house apparently had an old pool that the scouts swore could be filled and a large patio that looked over the bay. One senior boy started collecting a dare-fund to see him cliff-dive off the roof. Another went to Queens to buy hash and tequila.

The girls weren't required to do much to prepare except what they would do anyway: purchase new clothes and craft excuses for parents, make themselves up and worry about getting pregnant. All sorts of gossip and speculation preceded bonfires, for it was the time when anyone could experiment with anyone else, and most didn't miss the chance. Like the bookmakers at a Las Vegas casino, boys set odds on who could be gotten and who couldn't.

For Tony, a male seventh grader with no social ties and only a few meek acquaintances, Bonfire Night was something not even to know about, let alone participate in. But the rituals of Glen River High weren't exactly shrouded in secrecy. Adolescents don't operate that way. Secret societies can only be secret so long as bragging rights can't be auctioned off. Pranks, sexual conquests and stunts don't remain secrets for long when teenagers are in charge.

Besides, Tony had been planning to spend that night as he spent every Saturday night: eating silent TV dinners with his father and then retreating to his room, where he would find meaning in the dust motes along the wall. That is until Carter Moran, one of the junior scouts who was directly responsible for scoring the mansion for Bonfire Night, decided to publicize his good works.

He held court in the cafeteria, exaggerating tales of the selected site beyond wildest belief—not that there was any dire need to, the truth would have been impressive enough. But for Carter, a normally quiet and reserved eleventh grader, this was the first moment of school celebrity and he wasn't about to let it package itself.

Before long, the entire school knew of the decadent activities planned for Bonfire Night. Even the administration heard; but, as usual, they declined to get involved, adhering to the policy that activities off campus weren't the concern of the school but of the parents.

Tony McMahon knew that Patricia and Koosh would be intimately involved in Bonfire Night. That hadn't been hard to guess. But Tony wanted to know details, for he became almost excited that amidst the carnival atmosphere, amidst the flickering shadows of this bacchanal-to-be, something horrible would happen. The small boy who had worried that his beloved beachcomber was being swept off her feet by a linebacker was now hoping for orgiastic rites and pandemonium. He felt only in such a cataclysm would the relationship be sundered.

Of course, now that he predicted destruction, he wanted to witness it. Immediately he began to plan for the fateful night, checking that his father had plenty of liquor on hand so that he would pass out and Tony could sneak from the house unobserved. The main problem was how to get to the mansion. He had no means of transportation and was too young to know friends with cars. This was a major problem, but one he knew he could solve given time.

One night, lying in bed, he came up with the answer. He had a stash of fireworks left over from last year's July Fourth—mild items like bottle rockets and sparklers that he'd bought with money from his aunt. He would offer them as tribute. The next day, he watched lacrosse practice, fifty paces behind Patricia, as usual. As the players strolled from the field after the final whistle, he approached Carter boldly and, squeezing his small hands into fists to gather courage, said he had fireworks to contribute to Bonfire Night providing he could get a ride there.

Carter, though prone to indiscretions of all sorts, knew he couldn't very well make such a deal. But he liked the idea of having some fireworks. It was an idea that had never occurred to anyone. And all manner of pyrotechnics would go well with the kerosene flames. But a small kid like this was out of the question. Toby Picks, this year's Bonfire King, would unsheath him if he knew he'd made that kind of a deal with a middle schooler. Yet, the thought of claiming credit for the fireworks convinced him. Who would really care if one little kid rode in the car with them? They could always kick him out once they got there.

So Tony had schemed an invitation. The scouts, who were to arrive early and set things up, would pick Tony up at seven on Saturday evening, providing he had a big bag of fireworks to show them.

He ran home and rushed to his closet to make sure his fireworks were still there. If his father had discovered them, then his stash would be gone. But no. Luckily it remained, right where he'd hidden it, in his old gym bag at the bottom of the closet. He pulled it out and poured the rockets and sparklers on the bed. It was a beautiful sight: the colorful cardboard and paper signifying nothing else if not excitement and something deliciously illicit. He looked at the pile approvingly. Here were the items that had gained him entry to Bonfire Night, the secret ritual of the older grades. How strange that popularity could come in such packaging, thought Tony. Power and popularity both, just because of some fireworks. And all the time he'd thought you had to have a certain amount of chips to be popular, when the only thing that counted was how you stacked them.

11

"Good lawyers, like good golfers, know where the break is," Barolo said, sitting cradling his Styrofoam cup of coffee in the prison visiting room. "I'm a goddamn good lawyer and I know every which way this green breaks, Tony. I know these courts as well as Palmer knows Pebble Beach. I know the doglegs, the sandtraps, the angles. I know the pansy prosecutor even. All right? We went to law school together at Pace. He's gay as a blade and that helps our case. Every little fucking bit helps it. Every little divot out of place. Well I'm the genius who figures out how to stick that divot back in—not only so no one notices—but so the next guy trips over it.

"How do you know a good lawyer? I'll tell you how. It's not the fancy cars or the European suits, and I got all that shit. But any limp dick can fake that. A good lawyer, Jesus—a real fucking good lawyer is a piece of work. He keeps your attention. Look at you, Tony. You haven't blinked once since you came in here. Why's that? 'Cause I own you the same way I own the jury five minutes after walking into a courtroom. I make love to that jury. They don't know it. Some of them haven't been fucked for years, so how would they know it? I'll take an old lady whose biggest thrill is clipping coupons and watching lousy soap operas. I'll take a forty-year-old pig of a guy with a gut bigger than mine who jacks off to kiddy porn in his spare time. I'll take a nineteen-year-old virgin who doesn't even know what a jury is. I'll take a crack-addict pimp who got on the rolls through a fluke. I'll take all those fuckers and make love to them like they've never been made love to. I'm just that good.

"It's seduction, plain and simple. I date them, I stare them down, I rub their backs, I give them attention, I finger them, I get them wet, I lick their asses, then I fuck them so hard, they only want more. By then the case is over. No time even for a hug. I'm on to the next lover. But by then, Tony, you're sprung. You're a free man.

"What decides it all for me is this pansy prosecutor jerking off to some circumstantial fuck-letter he's calling a case. No one sends someone away for life for a letter. This guy is so dumb I don't even know how he ended up at the DA's. He's the kind of guy you'd never think in a million years would have even passed the bar. But who gives a shit. I don't.

"You're going to tell me everything. Pretend I'm your shrink or your lover. Whisper sweet nothings in my ear. Tell me you love it harder, softer. But tell me every fucking thing about that night and the nights before that night: what you did with Patricia, every fucking thing, whether you loved her, what you both did for kicks; tell me about your childhood, your father, your mother, your dog; tell me every minute of that night, what you ate at the diner, what the waitress smelled like.

"Tony, it's like golf, I said that. It's like fucking, I said that, too. A case is nothing without the game. Without one person winning, the other losing. Without one losing confidence and going limp, the other getting hard as a rod and diving in for more.

"When I was in law school they taught me cases, threw books at me. We went through all the regular bullshit. But I knew all along all that crap didn't make a difference for me. I wanted to get into that courtroom and fuck them dry. I knew that's how you did it, even then. I knew. I got instinct. I learned it on the streets, like you—I didn't learn it from a textbook, like the pansy prosecutor.

"Let me explain it to you. Criminal law, that is. I got a friend, a criminal lawyer in Miami—big drug cases, clients with money spilling out of their white linen suit pockets. All cash. And my friend was raking it in, OK? Condo on South Beach, giant house in Manalapan right on the water. So he's got these clients all the time. I was down visiting with him once. I asked him about his game. He said to me, he said, 'Ralph, I used to think it was all a game. But I can't do it anymore. I'm sitting here thinking now about the real shit that goes down. It's not a game. It can't be a game.'

"What do you think happened, Tony? Well, he lost his first case the next day. This guy had never lost a fucking case in fourteen years and the next day he drops one like a big dump. Crisis of confidence. It happens. You start thinking of it as anything else, you lose it. It's a game, Tony. Baby, you'll love it as much as I do."

"Ralph, I'm not guilty."

"Tony, if I ask you whether your sister's a virgin, what do you say?"

"I say I don't have a sister."

Barolo slammed his fist on the table. "Fuck that! Pretend you do. I'm giving you a lesson here. Again, let's say we're in a titty bar and I ask you if your fifteen-year-old sister's a virgin and you say yes."

"OK."

"And I say I want her, and you ask how much."

"OK."

"And I give you a hundred and you give me your sister that night."

"OK."

"And she bleeds."

"OK."

"Then how will I ever know if you were telling the truth? She could be a virgin—then again, maybe she's just menstrual. You see, truth doesn't fucking count. Reality counts. You got that, Tony baby? Do me a favor and get it before the trial."

12

The day of the big night threatened rain. Tony worried that his usefulness would be gone if it stormed, for he knew Bonfire Night would be held with or without rain, with or without fires—and certainly, with or without him. All through classes he spent as much time gazing out at the sky as he did looking at Patricia. At home, he called the weather phone six times, something his father had forbidden him ever to do. The reports varied little from hour to hour, but Tony saw a pattern that would deliver him. Rain was still predicted, but he had faith in God and prayed for a small dry spell.

At six that evening, the clouds rolled off and the night promised to be clear and beautiful. Tony decided to celebrate by setting off a test rocket. He grabbed an old beer can from the trash and a pack of matches from the kitchen drawer. He rushed outside into the warm quiet of the front yard. To do it here in front of his own home would be too dangerous. His father might wake up with the noise. At the very least a neighbor would see him and report him. So he ran two blocks, to the Wolonski house down the street. He knew Wolonski lived alone and had a hearing aid that never worked. This would be the perfect place.

He stooped to set up the rocket, being sure to angle it out and across the road, and away from Wolonski's windows. The match lit effortlessly in the stillness of the balmy night. The acrid smell pierced his nose and the rocket flew off in a satisfying streak of pyrotechnics, only to explode with a powerful pop high above. There was a second visual as well—a spidery network of yellow sinews that crested and then fell into the darkness. He was pleased. These were good rockets. He dashed between two bushes as windows along the street flew open. When the interest had died down, Tony ran home, just in time to see a blue Mustang screeching around the corner and stopping in front of his house. He grabbed his backpack and ran out to meet it. The car door flew open by way of greeting and he jumped aboard.

Inside, the scene was already boozy and boisterous. A huge kid with a crewcut that he'd never seen before was driving. He looked stoically calm, as if he'd been hired as a driver for the night and none of the festivities were to affect him. The kid across from him looked familiar to Tony. He had a thick scar like a hairlip that distorted his face. He had long hair, but dark and so greasy that it was matted to his forehead.

Carter sat in the back seat directly across from him. Tony waited to be addressed. But Carter was busy rolling a joint and he didn't seem to notice that Tony had climbed aboard. Finally, after he'd lit up and passed the joint along to the greasy one in the front seat, he turned to Tony.

"We saw you light that fucker up. Wicked job."

Tony had no idea how to converse with older kids like this, but he knew he was being complimented. "Thanks," he said, timidly, unsure whether to look at Carter or not. He decided to stare straight ahead.

"Let's see what you got."

"It's all in here." Tony unzipped his backpack and showed Carter the stash. He knew there was a lot, for he hadn't used any all year.

"Nice load. Tell you what." Carter paused to take another drag. "We're gonna let you get close to the bonfire. Right?"

Tony nodded. He sensed something was being negotiated but he wasn't sure what. He was happy enough to be included in the car ride and to feel wanted for his fireworks.

"So we'll drop you off outside the gate. Then we go in. At exactly eleven—you got a watch?"

Again Tony nodded.

"Aright. At eleven, you set off a bunch of rockets, right over the pool. By then we'll have everything burning. It'll be a fuckin' great explosion. Got it?"

"I got it." He was delighted to have such an important role and to be allowed to set off the rockets himself. The feeling of being a part of something was intoxicating. He'd rarely participated in stunts or games with other kids. He felt the same mixture of nausea and worthiness of purpose that a novice foot soldier feels upon being thrust to the front lines. His palms started to sweat as he considered his new responsibility. He rubbed them on his jeans. So this was what teenage life was like. Glorious, fraught with danger, and totally unforgiving if you screwed up. Well he wouldn't screw up. He'd set off the rockets at eleven, as planned, and perhaps even get to attend the bonfire. He smiled when he considered the extent of his own daring that had carried him to this point.

The roads were getting tighter and darker. The crewcut driver was still focused on the road. He had a beer in one fist, but seemed as sober as could be. Tony looked out the window in wonder at the tall trees and plush foliage. It was like the country here. He didn't know there were such places on Long Island, especially so close to Glen River. There were few houses and fewer cars. There weren't any streetlights, only the periodic cozy glow that filtered down from a home on the hill.

Soon the car slowed and came to a stop in front of a short driveway that ended in a gate crowned with barbed wire. Carter got out of the car and motioned for Tony to do so, too. Then the others followed and trained their flashlights on the gate.

Carter turned to Tony. "OK. We're gonna cut this. You go around the edge of this fence here—follow it all the way around to the bay side. Here, take this flashlight. Now you'll see the pool inside the gate on your right as you come around 'cause it's right near the fence. You park your ass in the trees there and wait till eleven. Then you light up. Might as well get them all set well ahead of time so that you can send 'em up quick. OK?"

"OK."

"Good. Now get out. Be looking for ya at eleven. And you can catch a ride home with us if you get the job done." That was the end of the briefing. Carter turned back to his friends to supervise the cutting of the fence. Tony noticed they'd already cut a small patch, presumably for one person to crawl through, and were now working to expand it. Carter noticed Tony dawdling. "I said move it."

He started around the perimeter of the fence. The torch Carter had given him was weak, and he could barely make out the logs and branches that stood in his way. It was slow going and he marveled at the obvious immensity of the estate. He could see just the silhouette of the mansion through the gate and shrubs, but it looked like a haunted house, imposing and huge.

Soon he heard what sounded like water and he realized he was coming up to the bay. Sure enough, he could make out the craggy rocks ahead and the lip of the sheer drop-off that stood behind it. He was thankful for having any flashlight at this point, for without it he might have gone off the cliff. The chain-link fence curled around and became a stone wall that separated the large patio from the rock face. He saw the gaping hole that was the dry pool. It was littered with leaves and other debris and didn't look too promising for a dip.

There was a small stone cottage to the right of the pool, like a guest house or servant's quarters. It had a small window on each end and no visible entrance. He assumed the door was on the other side, which faced the main house. This looked like as good a place as any to wait. He swept out a clear space on the ground and propped up the rockets one by one in the soft soil. Double-checking the angle, he determined that they would explode directly over the pool, just the way Carter wanted it. He looked at the array with pride. No one could have been trusted to accomplish this mission so well, he thought, savoring the deftness of his handiwork.

Now all there was to do was wait. It was only eight o'clock.

At ten, he stood to relieve the cramps in his legs and heard stray voices. They coalesced into chatter punctuated by laughter, and soon he saw a few boys pouring something into the pool. The harsh smell of kerosene wafted his way in the breezes. So the pool was to be the barbecue pit, not the swimming hole after all.

He knew that Carter had made sure to exclude him by keeping him outside the perimeter of the gate. That didn't worry him so much because it looked like he'd have a fine view of the festivities. He heard female voices and cocked his ears to pick up the high range of his beachcomber. Nothing. Soon music started to play.

A group of people gathered near the edge of the pool

and communally started to count down from ten. At zero, a massive flame licked out and savagely claimed the pool. Screams erupted and the whole patio was illuminated in a fanatical glow. Tony hadn't realized how many people ringed the poolside. He recognized many among the row of thrilled faces, orange with the kerosene fire.

Then he recalled his responsibilities and trained his flashlight on his watch. A quarter to eleven. That would give him just enough time to double-check the position of the rockets and crouch for the launch. He crawled back to his position in the patch of soil behind the pool house. And there, in the comparative quiet of the trees, bound by the taut anticipation of his task, he saw his beachcomber.

As she had on Jones Beach and then on the schoolbus, she appeared with the shock of an apparition. He was consistently wounded by her appearance. Even now, when he was so accustomed to her presence and could recall the very depth of the dimples in her cheeks, he was terrified. There in the window of the pool house she stood, swaying, almost but not quite dancing. The lights were on and he could see her with the colors and clarity of a feature film. She was dressed simply, in her designer jeans and a white T-shirt. The room had no furniture, only the naked bulb that illuminated it.

The door opened and Koosh walked in, framed by the orgy of flames that whipped up behind him—as if Lucifer come up from hell to party poolside. He carried a vodka bottle that he thrust toward Patricia. She waved it away and sat on the floor. Koosh pulled her up violently and led her through a few mock dance steps. She hung like a rag doll in his arms.

And then he started to undress her, to pull and paw at her T-shirt, fumbling miserably in his drunkenness, unable to do anything more than reach down her pants. Patricia froze, then sprung from his clutches and headed for the door. Koosh lumbered there, a step ahead of her on account of his long strides, and threw her to the ground. She screamed. At least Tony knew she did, from the outline of her lips, though the noise of it was swallowed by the savage crackling of the fire, the music and the laughter around the pool. Koosh lifted her and drew back his hand. He released it and slapped Patricia in the jaw. She fell to the ground and nursed herself. Her T-shirt was red. Koosh smothered her and tried to remove her jeans. He succeeded enough so that he started to undo his own pants and force his way upon her. She squirmed ferociously on the floor, finally able to spring free and out the door. Koosh fell onto his side, exhausted by his efforts.

Tony instinctively looked at his watch, though his hands shook and he had trouble making out the time. It was well past eleven and he sprung to position behind the rockets. He fumbled with the matches, trying six times before he got one lit. Then he ignited the first firecracker and sent it looping over the fence. The explosion came and he glimpsed the sparkling of the flare, hearing the coos and screams of delight that followed in its wake. After frantically lighting another match, he set about launching the rest. Soon a barrage of explosions and sparkling filled the night air.

Like the devil's apprentice, he lit up the sky and watched the hellfires devour the earth. While humans raped and pillaged, he sat at the controls alternately fascinated and horrified by the spectacle. He screamed. It was too much to bear. The sickness of the memory of Koosh upon his beachcomber made him ill. He wretched. But he couldn't help feeling that somehow that night had filled him with the mighty intoxicant of a power—a power that he couldn't have begun to explain. For he knew that after that night, though the fires would die in the oblivion of their own smoky end, he would never feel hopelessly weak again.

13

Ten pushups, ten situps, ten pushups, ten situps.

Ten pushups, ten situps, ten pushups, ten situps.

Ten pushups, ten situps, ten pushups, ten situps.

After the sixth set, he decided to open the letter. It was thicker than the last. Barolo had asked him just that day if he was corresponding with anyone. He'd said no because he didn't consider one letter back and forth correspondence. Now that Charlotte Celeste Hinney had replied, he supposed they were officially pen pals.

He used a towel to wipe the sweat from his chest and arms. Then he reclined on his bed, still breathing heavily from the exercise, and opened the letter slowly. There was the same lipstick kiss, the same perfumy smell, the same crisp paper. But no photos.

He read:

I'm so happy you wrote back. I was doing laundry when your letter came and it jumbled everything in my head, in a good way. It's funny you want pictures. I'm too shy to give them to you yet. But I'm sure that when the time comes I'll give you a couple. I can tell you about myself, though. I'm thin. A little too thin really. I sometimes feel awkward because of it. I wear no makeup, I don't like the look of it. I have a natural face. I wear flower print dresses and like to go swimming. I work in computer data entry. It bores me to tears. I have a brother. My parents are still alive. They live in Garden City too. We're not from money, so if you're looking for that, you better go somewhere else. Music is something I really love, rock mostly. I have a girlfriend who's really been getting me into new wave, rap and house. It's fun stuff. I do know what you look like, from the papers, and I think you're one of the most handsome men I've ever seen. Some day we'll meet each other for real and then we can talk. Maybe then I'll give you a real kiss, if I feel you deserve it.

Love,
C.

P.S. I'm glad to hear you didn't kill those people. Not that I'd have cared so much even if you'd done it. I imagine you would have had a good reason for it.

A good reason. Tony repeated the phrase: a *good reason, a good reason.* What was a good reason for murder? Self-defense, insanity, maybe. Not that these were really good reasons but they were certainly rationales—at least the law had said so. No, but those weren't really good reasons, were they? Revenge some people would consider a good reason. Vigilantism. Yes, people liked that. Killing to avenge a crime. That had its own special cachet of respectability in certain parts. How about fits of passion, desperation, misery, mania, depression? Were those good reasons?

What about provocation, enslavement by drugs, abusive families, abusive spouses, lack of sex, hypnotism? And then why not profiteering, religious fervor, hatred, duplicity, love, insurance policies, boredom, insecurity—good old greed?

Then there were reasons, like you needed to swipe either the grin or the sunglasses off some guy's face. Maybe you killed because somebody stole your favorite pair of hightops or looked the wrong way at your girlfriend; or perhaps sat on the hood of your Camaro or flipped you the bird; or even wore the wrong-colored shirt that day or joined the wrong health club; or was just in the classic wrong place at the classic wrong time.

These were the reasons people were killed. These were the reasons people murdered. And to Tony, after thinking it through for a while, they all seemed equally good, equally bad. Who was to claim that hightops were valueless—so much beneath honor and jihads in their solemn importance that they deserved less of a claim on human vitality? Why was it more worthy to kill someone to inherit his six-digit bank account than to make off with his Ray-Bans? Why more noble to defend your life than your Camaro?

To Tony, somehow, the boundaries were meaningless. He imagined the same shotgun blast either way. Good reasons he'd never found—not for murder or for even most things. Events seemed to run by and move along without reasons anyway. His ministry urged him to look to God for reasons. But he had long ago decided that God has no reasons. God has no intentions. God is satisfied without reasons and we should be too.

He wondered what Charlotte would consider a good reason? If he told her he killed the Carver family to get the two-year-old's hightops, he suspected she might be persuaded to think that a good reason. The idea made him quiver—for in it was power. He had power over Charlotte, he sensed from the first letter. He rocked from side to side in his prison bunk. That she had asked him and believed his answer—yet ventured to say that she would follow him anyway, even if he had killed and maimed and bloodied and slaughtered—that was power. For he could do no wrong. He could be a murderer, in fact or in fantasy, yet he was an idol, fit for worshiping all the same.

He sat up and penned a short reply:

Charlotte,

I can't think of any good reasons for killing someone. If I do, I'll let you know. Happy to hear you like swimming. Me too. When I get out of here, we'll go.

Signed,
Antonio McMahon, Inmate #90245

How nice it would be to swim, he thought. If he closed his eyes he could remember the sensation, though he hadn't been to a pool or a beach in years. He imagined the chill of the water and the foam of the surf. He imagined diving beneath—something he'd always been scared to so as a kid—then coming up for air.

Then he remembered a beach far, far away and sand castles and shells and a young girl with an outstretched hand. He couldn't see her face, but didn't need to. He heard her breathing, and that assured him it was her. It was a rhythmic breathing, so full of life that it must have been eternal. But then her heart exploded. Blood drenched him. He was blinded by blood. The sick sweetness of it matted his hair. Then the breathing stopped. And all there was was the sound of the surf.

14

He idled in the hallway until it was clear. Then he approached her locker and slid the note carefully through one of the slits in the top.

It said:

> Patricia,
>
> You don't know me but we met on the beach a long time ago. I wrecked your sand castle. Then I gave you a shell. I'm writing this note cause I saw everything that happened to you on bonfire night. If you need help, leave a note in my locker.
>
> Signed,
> Locker #146

After depositing the note, he looked both ways down the hall to make sure no one had witnessed him, and then hurried along.

He spent English class imagining her reaction. He fantasized that she would open her locker casually, as she always did, glancing quickly at the small mirror she'd affixed to the inside of the door. Then she would carefully set about exchanging her books after hanging her bag on the door as if on a back. The note would catch her by surprise, fluttering down gently right before she slammed the metal door. She would stoop to pick it up, hesitating to adjust her skirt before doing so. Finally, she would begin to read. The contents would surprise her visibly. Her eyes would widen, her face would flush. She would look around to make sure no one had witnessed that. Then she would fold the note back up and slide it into her math textbook for safekeeping.

He wanted desperately to appear heroic, to be sought after for help, to be needed by her in a way she had never needed anyone. He wanted to acquire the smallest bit of power over her that would somehow balance out the power she held over him. God had answered his prayers by providing the opportunity, but now he realized it was up to him to actually become a part of her life. Now was the time.

He never considered that she would feel threatened by the note or feel blackmailed. He never imagined that somehow she would be angered or confused by the overture of help. It was beyond his ken to realize that she would become crippled with fright at the thought of Koosh's violence becoming public knowledge. On the contrary, he assumed she wanted someone to talk to about her experience. And he imagined he would provide the ear.

For days he checked his locker after every period, especially after not seeing Patricia for a couple of hours. He always did this carefully, for he knew that she might be lurking around a corner, watching. And he didn't want her to know who he was. At least not yet.

But there was never anything. Though he'd cleaned out all stray papers and scraps so that he wouldn't miss her reply, the bottom was always as empty as he'd left it, and he began to worry. He figured she was wary since she had no idea who he was. He considered dropping her another note, a more detailed one with his name and photograph. But then he decided against it. He would be too embarrassed to pass her in the halls and see her in class after such a bold act. The anonymity of a Peeping Tom was what he craved. He'd experienced it that night at the bonfire.

One day, in just the manner he'd imagined it to happen to Patricia, a note spilled onto the floor as he opened his locker. So stunned was he that he couldn't bring himself to touch it. Through the bell of the next class he stared at it. Then he gripped it gingerly, as though it might be booby-trapped, and rushed off to class. He ignored the lesson and spread the letter on his desk. This was a dangerous act because Mrs. Ruttenburn, the natural sciences teacher, was fond of confiscating notes and reading them aloud—and he sat, as was his custom, two rows behind

Patricia. But he had to take the chance, such was the allure.

It read:

> *Dear Locker #146,*
>
> *I don't remember any sand castles, shells or beaches. I also don't remember bonfire night. Tell me everything you know quick. Don't leave out a thing.*
>
> *Thanks,*
> *P.*

He took the note outside to the field and held it to the sun. He didn't understand why she didn't recall anything. The beach he hadn't expected her to—but Bonfire Night? Well, she was probably drunk. With his peculiar brand of naiveté, he assumed that Bonfire Night for Patricia was probably a drunken blur, unconnected to memory.

He wasn't sure where he stood now. He felt guilty now that he had spurred her interest in a horrible event that she wouldn't have remembered otherwise. He decided he would write her a short note, fictionalizing what had happened and making it far more benign. What poor fortune, he thought as he went to sleep that night.

For Tony, in trying to be a white knight, realized he had found a damsel, not in distress, but in denial.

15

"Fucking motive, fucking means. You got it, baby. I love it, Tony. No one can get you out of this hole except me." Barolo leaned so close that Tony tasted the lawyer's lunch. "Did you hear that? No one—not one fucking one—can get you out of this hole except me. How does that feel?"

"As bad as can be."

"I thought so," Barolo laughed.

"What do we do now?"

"We figure this thing out, from minute one. Like I said last time, you pretend you're on your shrink's big couch. You tell me everything and I listen."

"Where do I begin?"

Barolo looked up at the ceiling. He brushed an imaginary piece of lint from his impeccable Armani suit, then fiddled with his French cuffs. "Begin with your night— your night that night, *the* night."

"I was working my shift at the Anchor 'n Sail—"

"Seafood?"

"Of course, seafood."

"Chowder on the menu that night?"

"Yeah, I guess. We got clam and seafood chowder every night. Why's that important?"

Barolo sneered. "Maybe 'cause I want to eat there on your fucking night off. Maybe 'cause I hate fish. Maybe 'cause I like to imagine a big boy like you spearing lobsters. Let's get one thing straight, Tony. Don't fucking ask me why I ask anything? Okay? I mean it gets down to basic things. I'm not a jerk. I ask what's got to be asked. I'm smart that way." Barolo paused to look Tony in the eye. "What would you do if I told you the police found a T-shirt with both blood and traces of clam chowder on it? How would you feel about that? Do you think that might help your case?"

Tony stared at Barolo. He could never tell if the Dictator was bluffing or dead serious, so mercurial was his manner. "I would think that's bad news."

"That's right, Tony. That's bad fucking news. You're a smart kid. The prosecutor has a T-shirt with goddamn Carver blood plastered on one side and Anchor 'n Sail chowder stains on the other. How do you like that? Do you think he picked it up at a novelty shop in Times Square— along with his *Kiss Me I'm Polish* T-shirt? He runs that by me yesterday to try to bully us into a deal. How does that feel, Tony?"

Tony was silent.

"That doesn't feel good, does it? So I ask you if the

Anchor 'n Sail served chowder that night. Because you see, in a murder trial, these pansies will throw it all at you. They'll hold up your undies with chowder stains and point at you and say 'He did it.' My job is to throw that shit back in their faces."

"That'll be some neat trick."

"That's right, Tony. Now you're thinking. Neat tricks. I like those. Now how about I ask you if you're positive chowder was on the menu every night? That you're sure they didn't alternate the lobster bisque that one night. Or how about I ask you if the chef gets lazy and doesn't make a new batch for dinner sometimes? Or maybe I ask you if you wear a uniform to work, something over a T-shirt? I mean how the fuck do you get chowder on your T-shirt when you wait tables in a restaurant. I know this place ain't no four-star place but I bet you don't serve your customers in T-shirts with your fucking beer bellies hanging out. Am I right? Maybe I drag in another lab freak who testifies that you can't isolate clam chowder off a T-shirt—that it could be half a dozen other things like jizz or mayonnaise or Jack Daniels. Maybe I prove the T-shirt belonged to Kirk Carver, that it had the same label of every other fucking undershirt in his closet. Maybe I just give it up to the prosecutor and tell the jury, 'If you want to convict this kid on a fucking clam chowder stain, be my guest. You judge him, but God will judge you.' "

"I do wear an apron," said Tony finally.

"OK, then. You wear an apron at work?"

"That's right. And a button-down shirt underneath."

"OK. And a T-shirt under all that?"

"Yes."

"OK. And all the waiters wear the same thing?"

"Yes."

"And when you arrive at work, what happens?"

"You punch the clock, you go to your locker in the basement, you change."

"From your street clothes to your fancy button-down thing and your prissy apron?"

"It's not fancy. Just a white, button-down shirt—"

"Whatever. What are your street clothes?"

"Well, I guess it depends on the weather. I guess that night I was wearing a T-shirt and my windbreaker."

"OK. You walk in with a T-shirt and windbreaker and—"

"And I guess jeans. And so I change to my black cotton pants and put the button-down over the T-shirt and then the apron over the button-down."

"And then?"

"And then we set up, wait tables, collect the tips, clean up and go home."

"Break it down for me. Anything unusual happen that night?"

"What do you mean?"

"I mean what I said. Anything unusual happen that night that you can remember?"

"What do you consider unusual?"

"Jesus Christ, Tony, are you dense." Barolo spat on the floor. "What's unusual. Let's see. Like did a big-titted girl dance nude on the tables? Did an old man have a stroke and die at the salad bar? Did the fucking manager give midnight mass to the maître d'?"

"Nothing like that."

"OK. Now when you leave and change back, what happens? Break it down for me. Go slow."

"Well, I go to change. I take off the apron and throw it in the laundry bin for cleaning. Then I take off the black pants and put those in the locker. I put the jeans on, then I go. I get in my car and start out for—"

"What about the button-down?"

"What about it?"

"Are you wearing it? Do you put it back in the locker?"

"No I probably wear it out. I usually just wear it home if it's dirty so I can clean it. The restaurant doesn't launder your personal items, only aprons, tablecloths, that kind of thing."

"I don't get it. It was in the locker to begin with. You changed into it. If you take this stuff home to clean, how the fuck does it get back in your locker. Magic?"

"No, I guess I brought it in my gym bag. I guess I didn't get it out of the locker. I never pay attention to these details. You just do this stuff, you don't think about it."

Barolo finally looked up, over the rims of his glasses. "I don't like that fucking attitude, Tony. I want you to think of every fucking thing. You got that. Every fucking thing. This ain't nursery school where you can slobber all over yourself, smear your shit on a canvas and then be called a genius. I'm not your mommy. I want facts. And you keep shitting all over yourself."

"Well, I guess I bring it in my gym bag—"

"What else do you keep in there—in the gym bag?"

"I don't know. Not much. Usually the paper, my wallet, car keys—because I don't like to have that stuff on me when I'm working—sometimes the shirt, a pack of gum, that's about it."

"So you wear the shirt out the door. Why not put it in the bag? I mean that's how you brought it in. Why not put it back in the bag?"

"Just easier to wear it, I guess. I'm usually so tired by—"

"So you get in your car in your button-down and jeans, is it? What about the windbreaker."

"Oh yeah, I wear that, of course, over everything. It was pretty cold that night, as I recall."

"You get that out of the gym bag?"

"Yeah."

"And the gym bag stays in your locker during the shift?"

"Yeah."

"And the locker stays locked with a padlock until you open it?"

"Actually, it's a combination lock. Only I know the combo."

"Then you get your gym bag, put on your windbreaker, lock the locker, go out to your car and go, am I right?"

Tony nodded.

"Don't you punch out?"

"Oh yeah, of course."

"So that night, what time do you punch out?"

"Eleven my shift ends. I leave about eleven-thirty usually. That night I'm sure it was the same as always."

"And the time clock would give that to us?"

"I guess."

"Has anyone ever fudged the time clock?"

"No way. We've all tried to figure ways to do that, believe me. Not that our hourly wage is so great—but we've toyed with the idea. Besides, they know any time clocked after midnight for a waiter has to be bullshit."

"So you punch the clock at eleven-thirty. You sure it wasn't eleven-ten that night? Or maybe eleven-forty?"

"It was eleven-thirty."

Barolo opened his file, paused to put on his glasses and glanced down. "Anchor 'n Sail says you punched out at ten-fifty-one that night, nine minutes before your shift officially ended." Barolo didn't look up. He was still staring at his notes. Then he raised his brow slightly. "Now forgive me if I appear pushy, Tony baby, but let me put it, well, as politely as I possibly can: Why the fuck did you leave your shift nine minutes early on a night that a murder of which you're accused took place about forty-five minutes away from the Anchor 'n Sail, according to the coroner's best guess, between eleven-thirty and twelve-thirty?"

Tony shook his head.

Barolo stared at him directly. Tony had never seen a stare like that. It had no conception of itself. "Do you have a good reason for that, do you think?"

"No, I probably don't."

"I didn't think that you did."

16

Two days later a new note was in his locker, a reply to his latest communiqué:

> *Dear Locker #146,*
>
> *I know you're lying when you say now you don't remember what happened on bonfire night. You better tell me what you know right away. I don't want to tell Koosh about this.*
>
> *Thanks,*
> *P.*
>
> *P.S. No one better know about all this stuff except you and me. Whoever you are, you'll be sorry if you tell.*

This note disturbed Tony. The threats saddened him. For he realized he'd been wrong about Patricia. She remembered everything. Yet, she was so worried the gossip would spread that she was manipulating him into telling what he knew. This duplicity first angered, then heartened him. He realized that the power he wielded had just increased exponentially.

What's more, the threat about Koosh was clearly a bluff. He could read that between the lines. Patricia's principal concern was that Koosh would find out someone else knew and suspect her of informing.

Like a tactician, he set about planning his next move—so obsessively that he was still lost in thought and disappointment when Mrs. Ruttenburn called his name for the third time.

"Tony McMahon!"

He came to. The class's eyes were on him. "Yes, Mrs. Ruttenburn?"

"It appears your attention is less than with us today, Mr. McMahon. What is going on? Please do tell the class."

"I'm sorry, Mrs. Ruttenburn." He knew he had to account for the note immediately. She had spied it with her hawk eyes, and he'd made the mistake of trying to fold it and stick it under his lab notes while she addressed him. He set his clocks on different speeds and tried to quell the panic which threatened to seize his throat. But he couldn't. His vocal cords were as if caulked shut.

"What is that you just tucked under your lab report, Antonio McMahon? It didn't look like scientific data to me."

"It's not," he said, stalling for time.

"What is it?" Mrs. Ruttenburn was excited now. She

took two steps from her desk and stared down at him. He felt as though their adrenaline was being drawn from the same gland, so close were they now and so palpable the tension. Here was a bona fide bust coming. She was going to draw it out to the best of her cowardly abilities and for the most dramatic potential of humiliation.

Tony glanced at Patricia. She, like everyone else in the class, was staring at him with a typically teenage amalgam of camaraderie and malicious glee. It was the first time she had ever looked at him since that day on Jones Beach. He was smitten. They were locked in a mutual gaze that rearranged his vertebrae by its very intensity. But then the corners of her mouth, which he had always admired for their pertness and expression, dipped from a mild smile into a worried frown. Her thumbnail moved up to her lip. Her face blanched. For at that moment she knew—she knew he was Locker #146. There was no question. All of a sudden his battle was her battle, and he felt a thrill of pride and union as their destinies became joined in such a strange way. It gave him courage.

He turned to look at Mrs. Ruttenburn. "It's official business." This was a risky wager, for Mrs. Ruttenburn was the type to scrutinize a claim like that. But he hoped she would do that privately, after class. He looked quickly at Patricia. She was pale and biting her nail feverishly.

"Is it, Tony? Would you like to read it to the class, or shall I?"

It was the moment of crisis, yet rarely in his life had he felt so confident, so controlled, so proud, so heroic. For he was defending his beachcomber as well as himself. The thrill pushed him onward. He had an idea—something he'd gotten from a movie once. "This note is private business. I'm sorry for taking it out in class, but it's not to be read aloud."

This inspired Mrs. Ruttenburn to new heights of sadistic drama. Her mouth widened into a broad, hideous, sarcastic smile. "Oh! Forgive us. God Almighty! It's *not to be read aloud*," she mimicked him with a sickly whine. She turned to the class and paused for full effect. "Did you hear that, class? *It's not to be read aloud.*" She turned back to Tony. "We're so sorry, Mr. McMahon, for disturbing your privacy. Maybe you shouldn't allow your private business to mix with your classroom work. Did that ever occur to you?"

He had never seen Mrs. Ruttenburn quite so flushed. Spittle flew from her mouth with the *p*'s in *privacy* and *private.* She had always hated him, but never had the venom glands been so primed. "Mrs. Ruttenburn, it has to do with another person. It wouldn't be fair to them if I read it aloud." He didn't dare look at Patricia.

"Let me be the judge of that. Please hand me the note."

"I'm sorry. I can't," said Tony tightening his hold on the small piece of paper.

Mrs. Ruttenburn hadn't counted on this much resistance. Never had someone so outrageously abused her authority publicly. Her voice quavered. "I said, hand me the note."

"I won't." Tony felt at that moment so omnipotent, so

superior to Mrs. Ruttenburn and the whole lot of snivel-
ing classroom toadies, that he felt he could have done anything then: could have sprinted for miles, could have staged
a revolution, could have saved his father from liquor, could
have asked out Patricia Macchiato.

Mrs. Ruttenburn stepped closer to him. "Give it to me,
or I will take it. Did you hear me?" Her voice broke in half
along with her confidence. The class was spellbound.
Never had a room been so quiet in the history of the Glen
River school system.

"I won't," Tony repeated. Mrs. Ruttenburn reached to
take the note. For this, Tony had prepared. In one crisp
motion he snapped the paper into a small ball and popped
it in his mouth. He concentrated on swallowing it, con-
vulsing his tongue and throat muscles to make sure he'd
completed the task.

The class roared fanatically with delight. So much so
that Mr. Hillson, the history teacher next door, rushed
into the room and discovered Mrs. Ruttenburn standing
above Tony. She was gripping his arm to the point of pain
but Tony could never have felt pain at that moment.

Mr. Hillson, upon hearing Mrs. Ruttenburn's nearly
tearful explanation, grabbed Tony by the armpits and
rooted him from the chair. Then he wrenched Tony's arm
behind his back and marched him from the room—but
not so quickly that Tony wasn't able to glance at Patricia.
She smiled broadly. And the image of that smile he would
carry with him for the rest of his life.

17

If he could have, he would have preached to a congregation. Lacking a congregation, he would have gladly preached to the choir. But without even a choir, he had only one option—he preached to his fellow inmates.

In the dream, Tony stood in his cell before an imaginary podium in an imaginary pulpit and looked along the prison corridor at his unlikely parishioners. How sinful they looked, he thought, with their tattoos and skin-heads and muscle-bound bodies. How decadent was all that moaning and sleeping and inattention they lavished upon the proceedings. With hellfire he would've liked to scatter them all and chase them, like moneychangers, from the temple. He began, slowly, with preacherly deliberation—a model, he thought, of oratorical power:

And God grabbed Abraham and told him to take Isaac up on the mountaintop to kill him there. And Abraham believed in God so he did that. But really he didn't want to kill his one son. He was waiting for something, anything from God so that he wouldn't have to do it. Abraham was just hoping that—

Shut up, motherfucker. Shut up, preacher boy. Faggot. Woman.

That was to be expected he thought, this heckling from such lost souls. He continued:

Abraham was just hoping that God would tell him to stop. He was begging God to keep him from doing this horrible thing that—

Did you hear me, you queer fuck? I'm gonna fuck your head so silly if you don't fucking shut up. Woman. Preaching faggot.

It was the hour before lights out, and technically he wasn't supposed to be talking, but the mood had struck him so he'd brought out his Bible and composed a few thoughts. He forgave his flock. They knew not what they said:

But God would not stop him. Abraham raised the machete. He began to swing the blade. Time ceased. He was waiting, just waiting for anything that—

Identify yourself, queer. That's right, wifey. You're going to get the Bible up your fucking ass. Fag.

Preacher boy. Come preach in my hole, you silly fuck. Hooooooooot! Hooooooooot! I'll teach you a thing or two about religion.

Now the congregants were even more restless.

Hooooooot! Hoooooooooot! Give me a blowjob, preacher boy! Suck my balls, preacher boy! Come here, Isaac. Give your daddy all it takes. Hey, preacher boy, I'll give you a pack of lites for a quickie. Bring your big Bible! Play like any priest!

The laughter was building. More and more hecklers chimed in. This was the type of challenge the Ministry had warned him of. He would proceed. He raised his voice many decibels:

And the word never came. God was letting Abraham down. He stood over his son, with the big machete. He was going to kill his only son. What was God going to do? There had to be a better way. Abraham remembered his life with Sarah and the times they spent in the tent. He thought of his beautiful son, Isaac, whom he loved more than anything in the great big desert where they lived.

What could he—

Guard! Guard! Preacher boy wants to slip out! Lock him in solitary. Lock the queer! Yeah, lock the fucking queer. Lock him!

A chant began, a hideous chant that built to a deafening crescendo:

Lock the queer! Lock the queer! Lock the queer! Lock the queer! Lock the queer! Lock the queer!

Over and over again. Then Tony wailed, a sickening, blood-curdling wail that cut through the chanting and silenced his flock:

Lisehhhhhhhhhhhhnnnnnnnnnnnnnnn! Listen to me! Listen to me! I'm telling you the story of your lives!

There was silence. They'd decided to listen for a moment. He continued:

And Abraham lowered the knife. What else was there to do? No one, not even God had told him not to. No one had stopped him. He cleanly cut his son's head off and it rolled in a bloody heap onto his right foot.

There was silence. Then one congregant spoke, in barely a hoarse whisper that carried easily in the sudden stillness:

You're one sick puppy, preacher boy.

With a loud clang, the lights went out.

18

The inner circle was composed of the leaders, their cronies, co-conspirators and lieutenants. Outside of that circle were other groups of varying status. Within these groups, too, were simple hierarchies: leader, linchpins, lackeys. Each group had its own agenda. One rarely, if ever, mixed with the other socially—unless forced to by one's parents. For the above is a description neither of political parties in the old Iron Curtain nor of kinship patterns in African tribes—but rather of middle-school social life in Glen River.

First and foremost was the inner circle: *the group.* No one had ever bothered to give *the group* a name. It was rarely referred to even by those two words. There was no need to tag it. Everyone knew who was in *the group.* They were the ones with the right taste and the right lingo, the right talents and the right way. Every school has such a clique. Glen River's *group* was the same animal. No one had ever questioned it. No one ever would.

To figure out why one was a member of the group was a bit like trying to understand why some people are monarchs, spending their days on plush settees with courtiers and concubines, while others are serfs, tilling the land with infectious boils in lice-ridden hair shirts. How one became a member of the group was a mystery that not even the most astute school psychologist could have determined.

A casual observer would have jumped to some hasty conclusions. That, for example, a skateboard, the new locomotive breakthrough at the time, was the key to group membership. But there were kids who bought skateboards with just such hopes, only to find themselves skating home alone every day without a prayer of belonging. Some might have guessed that a concert T-shirt from the right band was the passport. All too many had made that mistake as well, only to spend forty on the scalped ticket and twenty on the T-shirt, then to come to school sixty dollars poorer and no more popular. Athletic prowess was always assumed to be a good bet for membership, but of course, one can't buy that, and even if one could, there were plenty of athletes who commanded some respect, and yet, after the final whistle, somehow faded into obscurity.

No, admission to the group was not something that could be predicted with a Rorschach test, like sociopathology or a propensity for anorexia—not something that could be plotted on a curve of probability or expressed as a ratio like a batting average. At the beginning of the year when a new kid would arrive, everyone would know within a day or two that he or she was *in*. There was no initiation, no hazing, no board meeting, no democratic vote, no caucus, no talk about it. But somehow the kid was in. Everybody knew it and that was that. Just as easily it became known that a kid was *out*. This was not worthy of noting. There was no proclamation, no press release, no humiliating handshake of farewell, no catcalls or physical branding. Yet, the kid was out and everyone knew that he or she would never have a happy life—at least not within the halls of Glen River Middle School.

Not that this group was the be-all and end-all. Not at all. For membership in *the group* in *middle school* was only preparation and training for *the group* in *upper school*. And this ultimate tenure was hard to come by. From one to the other there was some fall-off: Some kids lost status as they grew. Physical changes and adolescent volatility rendered them unable to cope. They lost favor and were dismissed. Again, the process was as scientific as a tarot reading.

There were also new recruits. And they came aboard with a special brand of disdain for the outsiders they'd left behind. No one could be more hateful and cruel to someone who was *out* than one who'd once been *out* and was now *in*. There was always the danger of being deported and thrown back to the mercy of those you'd taunted and been a traitor to. But most never considered the risk.

The lesser cliques formed as pockets of belonging for those who hadn't gained admission to the group. They were more specialized, admitting kids of similar hobbies or interests and claiming different school areas as turf. Whether the focus was Star Trek, drugs, DC comic books, or heavy metal rock, each group had its defining activity and attendant paraphernalia. Really just clusters of apathy channeled into another useless hobby, these cliques defied the loaded title "gang."

And then there were the loners. And Tony was one.

Those who couldn't fit in anywhere due to their wrong shoe size or bad breath or slow way of talking or scrawny frame or crippled sister or whatever other strange barometer, were cast outside the pale. No group would have them, and if asked, they would claim they would have no group—certainly, as a comedian used to say, no group that would have them. But it's the way of nature to have some outcasts on which the other groups base their selection process. And who'd be the first to interfere with Mother Nature? Not Glen River Middle School.

Tony had stayed where he was for some time. Bonfire Night hadn't served to propel him upwards. Carter, by now a revered member of the upper-school group, had forgotten him completely. Tony would've been almost content to stay in his reduced status except for one problem. As an outcast he could have no actual contact with

Patricia Macchiato. As a mate to one of the school's royal family, Patricia would never, could never, have deigned to talk to Tony in person. And so another note appeared in Tony's locker that afternoon, the day he returned from a three-day suspension due to his showdown with Mrs. Ruttenburn:

> *Dear Locker #146 (Tony),*
>
> *Yeah. I know who you are. And I know you know I know. That's OK. Thanks for eating the note. You looked funny doing it and you sure got your butt in trouble. But it got me out of a lot of explaining stuff. I can't talk to you cause you know Koosh would get mad if I talk to any other boys. But I figured I'd send you another note.*
>
> *Thanks,*
> *P.*

It thrilled Tony to see the way she'd written his name. He traced the tiny bubble letters with his fingernail, disbelieving that she could really know that particular sequence of the alphabet: *T-O-N-Y*. He repeated to himself silently, *She knows my name.* Then he jumped once and ran out the door and onto the field. It was raining. He danced there, ignoring the wet and the potential spectators from the classrooms overhead. *She knows my name, she knows my name, it's unreal, she knows my name!* He said it aloud once now, testing the sound of it in the June rain. *She knows my name!* He was beside himself with pride. *To be known by Patricia Macchiato. To be known by her. Holy shit! To be known by her.* He danced again—a little jig that took first one knee nearly to the chin and then the other.

Then came the cry from above.

"Look, there's Tony McMahon! His first day back and he's dancing in the rain like a loony! Look! Quick!"

He stopped suddenly and stood there watching the three or four faces peering down on him. The pelting water kept him from seeing them clearly, but he stared back anyway. Then a teacher's voice cried out in the distance and the faces disappeared.

So what, he decided. *She knows my name!* He danced again, this time kicking his knees higher in disdain for these fools who couldn't understand such happiness— ever—let alone experience it. He reread the note, then placed it under his shirt to protect it from blurring any further. *She knows my name!* Again the chorus rang in his head. How did he get to this point? That she addressed her letter to him by name. She knew who he was and she even thanked him. It's true, then: He *was* a hero for eating the note and upstaging Mrs. Ruttenburn. He relived that moment with a zest for every detail, particularly the moment of triumph when his and Patricia's eyes met. That moment alone he had pictured already one million times. But now this, to be named instead of nameless. This was too good to be true.

It didn't even bother Tony that Patricia had forbidden

contact between the two of them. And if anything, the new bond between them had served to push them farther apart. Just that morning they had entered class together and ignored each other so completely that Tony had passed over his usual chair two rows behind hers in favor of an obscure one in the back of the room. That class he reined in his eyes; for the first time ever he couldn't have told you which shoes she had on, whether her hair was in braids that day, which arm she rested her head on. For on that day he looked only down.

But he was happy. To be known by her was the thing. To communicate with her was reward enough and to keep it close, to have it as a secret between the two of them, was even juicier. He did another jig on his way to the cafeteria, where he planned to spend his free period penning a reply. *She knows me!*

He wrote:

> *Patricia,*
>
> *Thanks for your letter. It's OK that you can't talk to me. I think this is like talking only better. I'm glad you know who I am. And I'm glad I know who you are.*
>
> *Signed,*
> *Locker #146 (Tony)*

He looked over his handiwork before going to deposit the letter in her locker. He studied his name. The presence of it delighted him. He slowly drew an

X through "Locker #146." No need for that anymore. He would never, *ever* go by a number again—not so long as Patricia Macchiato could write out the letters: *T-O-N-Y.* No, not so long as she could do that.

19

Dear Inmate #90245,

As long as you're going to sign your letters with a number I fig-
ure I might as well call you by a number too. But I also like the
name Tony and think it looks nice written out like this TONY.
Don't you think that looks better than #90245? You probably
don't care either way what anyone calls you. I'm writing to tell
you something I should probably get off my chest sooner instead of
later. It's sort of a confession. I got a boyfriend who I'm sort of
serious with. He's a jerk but I have to admit he's all I got. Until
you get out at least. He's an electrician so he makes good money.
Not that I live with him or anything like that. It's just Ed buys
me nice things and we go to St. Thomas every winter. You'd like
him probably. He can be a nice guy but he's nothing like you. He's
not special like you are. He's never been accused of anything. He
wouldn't have the guts to deal with jail. He's really just a spoiled

kid from Manhasset anyway. But the thing that I really just need to get off my chest is something I just haven't told anyone. It's something I haven't even told my girlfriends cause I'm too scared. Here goes. Ed beats me sometimes. He can get rough when he's had too many drinks. But sometimes it doesn't even take drinking. He just loses it and comes after me. He slaps me around. Never too bad, really. But bad enough so that I have to make excuses the next day at work. Last time my supervisor got so suspicious she came up to me and asked me what happened. I just told her this totally crazy lie about falling over on my Nordic track and busting up my face on the metal sled part. What do you think I should do? I know he's an OK guy really. I think I used to love him but I don't anymore. Besides, I think I'm falling in love with you.

Give me a sign.

Love,
C.

It was the first official confession he'd received, and he would have been proud of it had it not been for the contents. As a minister, he had expected that lost souls would begin to flock to him, searching for spiritual guidance. And he had made a vow that he would accept their confessions with ultimate objectivity, sympathy and professionalism. What then to do with this, the very first?

He ripped it apart savagely and let the scraps flutter to the floor of the cell. God sometimes does not forgive, he thought to himself. He rolled over to go to sleep.

20

The day it happened they served macaroni and cheese at lunch, the lacrosse fields got watered, it broke ninety degrees, Alicia MacGuiness bloodied her big toe by trying to kick Billy Castleman in the shin and missing, a stray dog wandered into gym, Mr. Gurley canceled class on account of his toothache, and the ice cream truck arrived late.

Tony remembered every one of those details and then some. He recorded each meticulously in his diary under the underlined heading: *Things That Happened The Day Koosh and Patricia Broke Up.* It was a big day and he wanted to capture all the trivial occurrences that formed its fabric. He didn't know the exact moment when the bell tolled the end, though he would've liked to. He suspected it had happened somewhere between third and sixth periods, because it was during the latter that Patricia stumbled into class late, face red, swollen, and tearful, and held up a nurse's note to the teacher with a small hand.

The class had been prepared. During the five-minute break between bells, gossip had spread along the halls and up and down the stairwells. The older girls speculated that Koosh had finally come to his senses, realizing he couldn't become a senior and still have such a young girlfriend, while the younger girls figured Patricia had decided Koosh was a big jerk. The younger boys, except for Tony, were so indifferent as to spend those crucial five minutes flipping cards, oiling skateboards, or trading comic books—depending on their group affiliation. The older boys were silent, sworn to an instinctive code of secrecy by their allegiance to Koosh.

When Patricia came in crying, even within the harsh cellblocks of adolescence, there was no one who didn't feel some sympathy for her. It was clear that her life at Glen River would be so different from now on. By having ascended the social ladder so quickly, she had taken great risks and they had come to bear. She had already alienated most of the important girls. And without Koosh she was very little indeed. No one would forget the stuck-up way she had acted during those months. Such slights were not easily forgiven. More importantly, no boy would date her because the shadow of Koosh was too big to compete with and too threatening to walk behind. The sagest and kindest fortune-tellers predicted that Patricia had at least the advantage of the long summer looming ahead. Maybe eighth grade would push the seventh into obscurity, they suggested. But none really believed it.

How unfair, the feminists would have reflected had there been any at Glen River. For though Patricia would be branded for life, Koosh would be reincarnated as a newly eligible bachelor senior, one who could take his pick of many. Not that Koosh wouldn't suffer. He would have to choose a girlfriend quickly—the junior prom was in two weeks.

It wasn't only the students who noticed. Despite the faculty's attempt to look removed from petty student socializing, one or two had something or other at stake. Carol Dugan, Ph.D., M.S.W., had a vested interest in the proceedings. As school psychologist, she was well versed in the topic of Koosh and Patricia. In the middle of the year, Dr. Dugan had received numerous calls from seventh-grade mothers, worried that Patricia would start a quite unwholesome trend by dating an upper-school junior. Dr. Dugan had sought to quell these fears by suggesting that this was an aberration—not something likely to become faddish—and even if it weren't, it was certainly outside of the school's jurisdiction. Yet, stunned by the chord the issue had struck and fearing a flurry of lawsuits should middle-school daughters be routinely fondled by upper-school football players, she'd immediately filed a series of memos with her supervisor. The supervisor had warned her not to waste precious school resources on dictating romantic behavior while problems like drugs, drinking and pregnancy loomed so heavily. But Dr. Dugan had not been able to sell the same shifting of priorities to the parent body and had started hav-

ing gastrointestinal troubles. She was considering something over-the-counter, when she heard of the breakup.
While watering her office azaleas, the loud after-school
chatter of young girls drew her head out the window. She
listened intently for a minute and then went back to watering. *Well, thank goodness, that's that,* she thought with benign relief.

Coach Henley was also relieved. He'd been depending
on Koosh to step into the starting quarterback role that
next September since Ray Paglio, all-state passing leader,
would graduate that spring. Koosh had always been the
backup, but Henley knew that Koosh would need all his
concentration to keep track of playcalling, audibles and the
complicated aerial offense that Glen River liked to run.

He'd picked out Patricia as bad news from the beginning.
Any girl who at that age was running with sixteen-year-old
guys had to be bad news, thought Henley. Not that he
couldn't see the attraction on Koosh's part. Patricia was quite
a little number with her miniskirts and long hair and fey
looks this way and that. Had she been a few years older—
well a good bunch years older—he could've been tempted
himself, he once told his assistant coach. She's too old for
you, Henley, joked the assistant, who'd also been "confused"
by Patricia's sexual and overly mature bearing but was loathe
to admit it. The way Henley saw it, once Patricia started at-
tending games, Koosh's performance had gone downhill. He
was glad to have that temptress out of the picture.

Mr. Graves was worried. He'd heard of the breakup
while grading grammar quizzes in the faculty lounge. As

Patricia's young English teacher, he'd been the closest thing
to her confidant. She'd never discussed Koosh with him directly. Poetry assignments were the medium through which
she expressed her feelings: A sonnet or two rhymed their
way into a series of couplets on Koosh's arrogance; a haiku
lengthened into a lamentation on Koosh's cruelty; an experiment with ballad chronicled Koosh's physical abuse.
One read:

> *He makes me cry.*
> *He makes me bleed.*
> *He makes me hurt.*
> *Still I want him.*
> *Still I need him.*
> *Still I love him.*

Mr. Graves hadn't known what to do with the first
poem. He'd passed it off as the rumblings of emerging adolescence. When the second and third had the same themes,
and the fourth named Koosh directly, he decided to tell the
principal. Then the fifth poem, in haunting anticipation of
this move, concluded:

> *And if anyone tells anyone about my problems,*
> *I'm sure to kill myself as sure as day turns to night.*

That day he pulled Patricia aside after class and asked her
if she was in trouble. If so, did she want to talk to somebody? Never, was the answer to both questions.

After that Mr. Graves spent the first five minutes of every day weighing his options. His teaching certification had never prepared him for this possibility. Nor had his study of poems, plays and novels. Even less helpful had been all those faculty meetings devoted to topics like scheduling, parent conferences, and proper report card form. On instinct, he decided his hands were tied. Besides, it was probably all overdramatics—a little girl crying out for attention. But now that the little girl had been abandoned, he worried anew.

And then there was Tony.

Having recorded the final details in his diary, Tony thought how different life would be from now on. Once again would he ride the bus home with Patricia, once again would he follow her from place to place unfettered by her constant companion, once again would he be able to imagine her alone—always alone.

21

"People ask me what the perfect murder is. You know what I tell them?"

"What?"

"I tell them the perfect murder is the one I get you off of."

"That's a good answer."

"Fucking *right*. It's the *only* answer." Barolo adjusted his watch. He was forever tightening and loosening the fit on his substantial wrist. "It's the *only* answer. 'Cause there are no perfect fucking murders, not in real life. Some jackass is always thinking he'll pull it off—hoping against fucking hope that he'll be the one to knock off his wife to collect the insurance. You know what a guy like that does?"

"What?"

"He takes out a policy on her a week before. He buys a gun, forges a suicide note, shoots her in the head, puts the fucking gun in her hand, goes out for a beer with his buddies till dawn, comes home, calls the ambulance, cries a lot to the cops. What happens?"

"What?"

"He doesn't collect. Why? 'Cause the insurance doesn't pay on a suicide. Some shmuck, huh? Didn't read the fine print. That's your typical genius who plans the perfect murder. So what happens then? Well, the cops know he did it. It's obvious even to the fucking paramedics who come to take away the corpse. So they try to squeeze him."

"Was this a client of yours?"

"That's right. I sprung him in a second."

"How?"

"Well this guy comes to me crying. He won't admit what happened, but I know everything. He tells me the fucking story the same way he tells it to the cops. Won't budge. This guy is brain-dead. I'm talking fucking moronic, OK? I get out the insurance policy, show him the wording and tell him it'll save his life."

"How's that?"

"I convince the jury he's a decent, smart guy. His alibi is weak 'cause the time of death doesn't jive with his time with the buddies—not a big fucking surprise. But I convince them this guy was on top of things, that he kept the checking accounts, he did the taxes, he was the householder, he ran a business. All right, so what if it was a Burger King franchise—I tell them food services. They eat it up 'cause most of them are just like him. Then I ask them, I ask how the fuck does some asshole decide to murder his wife to collect the insurance and not know that it won't pay? I say to their faces, I ask: *Is he that stupid, is anyone that stupid, could you be that stupid?* I ask them, you want to tell me this guy, a good husband, a smart man like all of you folk, is *that* fucking brain-dead? Of course, all these jury jackasses would have or could have made the same mistake, they're that stupid. But none of them can admit that. It'd be like admitting that about themselves to say he'd done it. See I get them connecting, sympathizing with this guy so much they fucking *become* him. So they can't convict him. They don't *buy* the motive. I don't even put him on the stand 'cause he'd blow it. I just let them look at the fat guy with his puppy dog face. They just don't buy motive and without motive he walks. Acquitted on all counts."

"But with no insurance money."

"Not quite. I told you that this was the *perfect* murder. Well, I turn around and represent this guy against the insurance company and I show them the coroner's report— everything that says murder. Fucking lab rats knew it was murder 'cause of the angle of the shot. So everyone agrees it's murder. But now they just don't know who did it. 'Cause my guy's off and he can't be tried again under double jeopardy. But I get him the one-million-dollar insurance settlement and this bozo moves to Pompano Beach, buys a big house, marries again and lives happily ever after in style. The whole time this joker never fucking *admits* he did it, to me or to anyone. So I go with him. I *run* with him. I have *instinct*. I take my clients and *run* with them."

Tony lit a cigarette. He'd taken to smoking a lot in jail.

Barolo always brought him premium cigarettes, half of which Tony pawned for books or magazines, half of which he kept for himself. "And me? What are you thinking about me?"

Barolo laughed. "I told you. I move with my clients. I don't give a flying fuck whether they're guilty or not. Guilt, innocence doesn't interest me. That's not where the story is, that's not the sexy part. The sexy part is what you do with the jury. How you treat them, massage them, make love to them, twist them into submission, suck them dry. They couldn't give a damn whether you did it or not. They care only what you *mean* in terms of *their* lives. Are you *them*? If so, are you the type of them they could see themselves being? If so, you walk—only 'cause they fear for themselves. Everyone knows they could do these things that people do, that *you* do. They gotta know that you *are* them. Then they can't punish you 'cause they can't punish themselves."

"You didn't answer my question. What about how you think of me?"

"There are always two possibilities." Barolo held up a thumb and forefinger. "You did it or you didn't. Again, that's all for St. Peter and Lucifer to worry about. I deal with down here. I paint it for the jury however I want to. I may make you out to be whatever I want—whatever I know they need for themselves. You'll learn. There's no such thing as truth. Only stories—good and bad." Barolo frowned. "You like stories?"

Tony nodded.

"OK, 'cause whatever it is, it'll be a story at this point. You may think *you* at least know what really happened but you don't. It's all storybookland once it happens. I'll tell you a story and you'll see how you like it."

"OK."

"A guy loves a girl. She leads him on, makes him happy, then makes him crazy 'cause he's nuts about her. He loves her so much that he wants to own her. That's not her plan, though. This guy has nothing. He works in a restaurant. He's pretty much a bum. Not daddy's best bet for any marriage. She wants to marry rich. Want to hear the rest?"

"All right."

"He writes her letters, proposes to her, even buys her an engagement ring with money he saves up over the whole fucking year. But all this doesn't interest her. She's gold digging. She goes to parties, she social butterflies it, she hobnobs with the Gold Coast set. She's savvy, sexy, young—a charm. She has no problems. She gets a job with an auto dealership—secretary or something. One day she catches the eye of the owner who she just *happens* to know is *the* dealer in Long Island. How does this sound so far?"

"Keep going."

"Well, this girl, she knows what she's doing. Very soon she has Mr. Big Autodealership wrapped around her pretty pinkie. Soon she gets married on the fucking Sound with a live band, champagne and all the green-with-envy relatives from all over the Island.

"So these two move into a castle—an estate—the kind of place Mr. Minimum Wage didn't even know existed until he started driving by (only when Mr. Big Auto is at work or away on business, of course). They have all the fanciest things. Of course, right off the bat it's a shit marriage 'cause she's not really into the guy except for one reason. But as we all know, that's one pretty big reason, so she makes do. She wants the pearl necklace, she gets the pearl necklace—with pearls so fucking big, they look like ape *cojónes*. She wants the designer dresses, she gets the designer dresses—for price tags that most people find on Winnebagos. She wants the Ferrari Testarossa, she gets the Ferrari Testarossa—even though her husband sells German cars. She wants the weekend in Paris, she gets the weekend in Paris—even thought they have to go by fucking Concorde 'cause she hates to—"

"How'd you know that?"

"Struck a nerve, did I?" Barolo smiled.

"I'm just asking how you knew she hated to fly?"

"I do my homework. I tell you I'm a good fucking lawyer. Soon, I'll know more than you."

"About what really happened?"

"Like I said, what really happened isn't worth squat. What matters is what I say, here, over my piss coffee and your stinking cigarettes."

"So go on."

"So they have babies, these two. But they don't have babies without nannies and they don't have nannies without maids. And they don't have maids without gossip starting all over the place. Slaves talk. How else do they get by? So we got a bunch of talkers. One of these talkers wants to crucify the young suspect—just for the hell of it—maybe because she's an old spinster, or just a plain old bitch and doesn't have anything else to do. She tells the prosecutor that she saw him all the fucking time, coming over, sneaking between the sheets with the missus in the afternoon."

"What about the kids?"

"Getting to that. Hold on, Tony, you got lots of time. The kids, the usual: the kids grow up, the marriage grows apart. What do they say, sixty percent of marriages give up on the sex after the second kid comes along? I say that's conservative. When you add up the impotence, the fucking frigidity, the resentment, the diseases, the insults and the boredom, I'd say you're lucky to have ten couples in a hundred humping away happily by then.

"Anyway, the kids." Barolo sipped coffee. "The kids are fine enough. Good kids. Solid this, solid that. No weaklings born to a Carver. They aren't spoiled shitless—I mean these *are* fucking Protestants we're talking about. But need is a word they don't know. From the womb, nannies, new clothes, not a moment alone, nothing less than the best. Patricia picks out the wardrobes with care. How your kids dress is an extension of your whole fucking soul—or what passes for one in Hautucket Bay. So that's the kids."

"Get to what counts."

Barolo laughed. "I guess you mean the night."

"Well, that's the real story, isn't it?"

"I don't know about that. Show me any story and I say

it starts before the beginning—somewhere else—in a place that no one ever gets back to. Except me.

"But, Tony, I'm getting to that night, believe me. That's the kind of thing that I love to lead the jury through. Most criminal hotshot lawyers, they hate that part. The night or the day or the moment when it all happened: For them that's the part to hide from the jury, it's the part where, according to them, their client was out bowling with his buddies, or at home fucking his wife. Or if they can't think of a lousy alibi, they hate that part even more, 'cause then they have to pull a reasonable doubt out of some other hat—then that moment, the murderous fucking moment, becomes a nightmare for them. The best thing they can do for their client is shove it down the jury's throat that there's no connection between that moment and the guilty-looking bozo who's sitting next to them in court.

"But that's not enough. For juries you have to create another reality, one they live in all themselves. I create that. I do that. I fuck them with a fantasy. And that's all jurors want anyway. They want a clean, good story, one that makes sense—not that it has to be true. As I told you so many times that I'm getting hoarse over it, truth is most of the time less interesting—and it's always less important.

"So getting back to that night. I'll serenade you. You tell me what you think of *my* version."

"Go ahead."

"Kirk Carver is getting restless. His wife has stopped fucking him. His kids he doesn't know 'cause they're with nannies all the time and he's working too hard to notice. Business is bad, by the way. Carver BMW's sales have declined thirty percent in the year leading up to that night. Why? 'Cause the old man let greed suck him dry. He expanded too quick, took on too much debt, bought a chain of yogurt stores that went bust, wandered out of his league.

"Carver is scared. With revenue way down, he can't even cover the debt on the loser investments. Cash flow dries up, he's ready to snap. But what's really bothering Carver has nothing to do with what's fucking his business. It has to do with who's fucking his wife. What gets him is not what's in his balance sheets but what's in his bedsheets. He knows that his wife is acting different. He thinks some back-door man has the key. Little things tip him off, as they always do. He notices that her hairstyle changes; that she's got lingerie he never gave her; that she leaves the kids alone on weekends and drives to the club, only to never remember who she ran into there; that her kisses are a quick peck on the cheek; that her dresses barely squeak past her ass for the first time in five years; that she talks less and daydreams more; that she *hi honey*'s him more and whispers in his ear less. These are the things that come together like a jigsaw even more deadly than photos catching her in the act.

"He gets depressed, then pissed, then desperate. He hires a private dick who gets nowhere but it still bugs him. He considers killing the back-door man. But he's not stupid. He knows the problem's Patricia, not the born loser from the wrong side of the tracks who's tupping her. He gets a hold of a gun anyway. He buys it on the street so it can't be traced—a Smith & Wesson .38—a gun big enough to guarantee a clean, quick job. The guy who sold it to him, a piece of street scum named Stump, thinks he remembers Carver: He arrived in a big blue BMW and a sweatsuit and paid in small bills.

"So Carver buys the gun. The next morning he doesn't show at work, curious thing for a guy who hasn't missed a fucking day in two decades. He takes a long drive. A gas station attendant on Glen Cove Road remembers filling up the BMW. He remembers because the guy was so fucking nervous and nuts that he threw a twenty at him for five dollars of gas and then drove away without change. He drives all the way to Bridgehampton and back on the L.I.E. He goes to three or four convenience stores to buy coffee along the way. These fucking Pakistani cashiers remember him 'cause he didn't look like he needed more coffee—he was so high-strung he looked ready to kill. And he was. Almost.

"He gets back to Hautucket at night—maybe around midnight. Patricia's in the kitchen, shoving something in the microwave. He walks right up to her, tries to stroke her hair, even tenderly, as if to see if it's really true that she would never do the same. Annoyed, she shakes herself away and checks on the food. She doesn't bother to ask where he's been. Then he looks around at the huge kitchen with its two separate fucking islands, its state-of-the-art this and that, the real brick pizza oven that Patricia had demanded, the pricey copper pots and the silly appliances, and he feels dead. He feels as dead as he could ever feel. Then he makes up his mind. He walks out to the car and gets the gun out of the glove compartment. It's misty and dark, and he has a hard time finding his way along the gravel drive. And that's the last thought he ever has. And that's no bedtime story, Tony. But I'm not a fucking nursemaid—I'm a lawyer."

22

Little girls grow up. That's a truth as old as the wind. But what about little girls who are already grown up? What becomes of them when it's their turn? That was the question that faced Patricia Macchiato at the age of fourteen.

It's a question of metabolism, says the biologist. Too much growth, too soon, too quick is the result of a faulty mechanism—an internal clock set incorrectly: hormones askew, cellular respiration overtaxed, calories combusting like firecrackers. Nails spring like cataracts, hair shoots like silly string. Biology has rules, though. What grows quickly, dies quickly. Larvae develop overnight—then die in a fortnight. You can't fool nature. It's one cruel curve.

The priest says it's a balance between innocence and knowledge. The forbidden fruit should be declined as often as it's offered. Forget about the fact that Milton says a cloistered virtue isn't worth a damn. What about those virgins who no longer are, those Adams who've already tasted, those Edens that were moved to the banks of the Hudson from heaven? For them, the church allows salvation. But the price is undying faith—a tall order for the less-than-devoted.

To the psychologist, it's a question of stages. Everyone passes through them, though not at equal rates. Moving too quickly poses dangers: hasty transitions, fractured growth. And worst of all, arrested development. Getting trapped in a stage is a purgatory inhabited by what society calls emotional cripples. Here, death poses no worries. In fact, death is often a welcome release from the never-ending limbo of the soul. The clinicians call those things suicide and depression.

For Patricia, who was no theoretician, these things merely spelled out the prospect of a messy adolescence.

For Tony, who was no saint, these things spelled out his best chance.

He began to scribble:

Patricia,

Now that I know you and you know me (Locker #146—Tony) and you've been through some rough times I think we should talk. That is if you want to. If you're in the mood meet me in back of the Crackerbox where the dumpsters are after last class.

Though he'd gained an identity, he still felt safer behind a number. Though he'd gained the loss of a rival, he still felt safer pretending he had one. Though he'd finally stumbled upon an overture by which to confront Patricia, he wished that he hadn't.

And though he was in the middle of his Beginning Algebra final exam, he was writing a note to Patricia. He glanced down at the test momentarily. He knew he would fail if he didn't attend to at least a few of the problems. But all the xs and ys addled him beyond sensation. Algebra had never clicked with him. He'd been intrigued by the idea of letters that stood for numbers—or that could stand for any number—but somehow it was all too much for his young mind. He flipped through the pages; the test was as thick as his pencil. That decided it: not only would he fail, he would fail miserably. So miserably that he would probably have to repeat seventh grade—or even worse, be kicked out of school.

Suddenly the idea appealed to him. To be *kicked out*. He repeated the words under his breath, feeling the satisfying grip of the c and the k as they combined into such a harsh reality. It was definitely one of those words that sounded like what it meant. Kicked out. How would his father react? How would Patricia? She might not talk to him if he became a Glen River outcast.

Yet, without school, his life could really begin in earnest. Up until now, life had been fits and starts, bucks and dips, fretful lethargies and melancholy regrets. This couldn't be life, he'd often thought. Thus life hadn't started yet. Life would come when it was ready. He imagined it arriving with terrible premonitions: silver-gray storm clouds on the horizon, a humid calm, a cavernous moan. And then life would appear on a grand chariot with hurricane force, and sweep him away to that secret outpost that had forever eluded him.

Yes, school was in the way. There was no doubt about that. Exams, yellow buses, hall passes, sadistic nurses. The trappings of school were holding him back, preventing him from finding his way. He'd always suspected it. But as he sat in the last row of seats in the gymnasium and ignored his test paper and looked around at the small pliant bodies bent over their work with a useless intensity, he knew that all this was evil.

He turned to look at the boy next to him. It was Cecil Barnes. Cecil was a fellow outcast, probably due to his odd habit of allowing drool to dry and congeal at the corners of his mouth, his unfortunate name and his excessively diligent work habits. Tony watched Cecil flipping the pages, filling in the problems, scratching away on the scrap paper that had been supplied them—the paper on which he'd written Patricia. He watched for a good minute, marveling at Cecil's single-minded passion for those algebraic tangles. He watched until Cecil, with that middle-school jungle instinct for survival, noticed Tony's stare and hurriedly shielded his test from view.

To be kicked out. Life would surely begin then. How else could it happen? It wouldn't happen sitting here next to Cecil, who had by now contorted his whole torso into a cheat-proof screen by which to guard his answers. Tony turned back to his note and wrote:

We can talk about whatever's on your mind. I don't plan to be around Glen River much longer. I'm sitting in our algebra test right now and things are going bad as can be. So bad that I'm writing you this letter. You're at the front of the gym so I can't see you but I guess you're having about as much fun as I am. I'm thinking about what to do if they throw me out of here. Maybe I'll

That's where thoughts left him. He had no plans. Life would begin—but with what? Without school and with a newly found life, where would he go? What would he do? And with whom? He felt depressed.

Then he thought of a plan. An escape plan of sorts. A plan for the newly found life. He would run away—and he would take Patricia with him. Without all the silliness, without the teachers and the skateboards, the cafeteria lunches and the bonfire nights, without all of that, surely they could begin a real life together.

To start a *real*, real life, they'd probably have to leave Long Island. Tony suspected that real lives weren't lived there, though he'd never seen anyplace else and wasn't sure if they could be much better. If they left Long Island, they could go anywhere—to Africa, maybe. Or even to Italy. His history teacher had told him that in Italy there was a certain city where there were no cars, only boats. You went everywhere by river taxis and all the houses sat right in the water. What's more the city was sinking—slowly—but sinking. So that in hundreds of years everyone would be living all the time in boats. That sounded closer to real life than anything else—more so than Long Island anyway. Maybe they would go to the sinking city.

Or maybe they wouldn't. Because try as he might to think of a way to propose this journey to Patricia, he could only think of saying *Come with me*, and that didn't sound convincing.

He decided to finish the note ambiguously, without any mention of the impending journey or the great adventure into new life that awaited them both. Better such things be suspenseful anyway. And also better to tell her in person.

He signed off:

I don't know what I'll do really. Not yet. But please meet me in the back of the Crackerbox. Bye.

Signed,
Locker #146 (Tony)

He looked up at the big humming clock that hung on the far wall. Time was up. The proctor clapped her hands and started collecting the tests. He looked at his own empty pages. He would surely fail now. But he was excited at the prospect and he eagerly awaited the moment when he would turn in those pages, for that would be the beginning of the end that beckoned his new beginning.

Finally the proctor arrived: Mrs. Durham, the office secretary whom he barely knew but had heard stories about—about how bad her breath smelled and about how she liked to make kids wait especially long while waiting to talk to the head of the middle school. She collected his test booklet.

"Tony McMahon, where did you write your answers?"

A small group of students who had started out of the gym paused to watch what they sensed might be a small developing drama.

"There aren't any."

"There aren't any?"

"No."

"Well, just what were you doing for these past two hours besides failing your Beginning Algebra exam?"

He considered telling all of them, Mrs. Durham and the assembled students, about his discoveries and plans, about how they, the uninitiated, could continue to live their paltry half-lives, while he would have none of it. But he was learning that ideas are dangerous, especially dangerous ones, and it was better to keep such things to yourself.

"I don't know, Mrs. Durham. Time seemed to zip right by."

23

Between visits from Barolo there was very little to do. Tony passed the time by napping, reading the Bible on and off, and doing little cell chores like neatening up. He couldn't tolerate one of his three books out of place— couldn't bare to see his papers unaligned. With so little space to breathe, to live, to be, he needed everything just so. It became an obsession.

Sometimes, while reclining a yard away, he would notice a pair of underwear that he'd forgotten to put in his cubby. This could produce heart palpitations and such violent unrest that he would leap up to fold those briefs—and only then, sleep.

Lately, all sleep was devoted to dreams, and all dreams were devoted to the courtroom. The actual one loomed larger and larger, even though Barolo and the prosecutor were constantly pushing back the trial date through their parrying motions. Tony had initially tried to keep track of every jab, every feint, every sidestep, every rope-a-dope. But soon the rounds lost definition, and the bells he couldn't hear. He knew that Barolo was forever trying to suppress evidence, and the prosecutor was forever trying to undo Barolo. He'd been told that he had the right to attend all these pretrial proceedings, but he'd waived the right and so slept instead. Tony visited the judge's chambers in his dreams. There he pictured Barolo, a massive presence, currying favor with the black robes behind the big desk through smiles, gestures, jokes and the type of uncharacteristically proper language he reserved for such occasions. He pictured the prosecutor thin, conservatively dressed, dour and unamused, watching Barolo suspiciously.

Today he was awakened by the clang of the cell door next to his. The previous resident had been transferred the day before. In between they'd fumigated, and the stench of the chemical wash still infested the air. Tony sat up in bed and watched the newcomer enter. The door slid shut automatically. This new one looked Hispanic, dark cheeks, a freshly shaved head and face, and squat—strong. He hoped this one would be as talkative as Rabbit, the last, who'd never said a word until he said good-bye.

The new inmate looked over solemnly and sat on his bed. Tony never worried himself about these people. So far he'd had no major problems. Accused of first-degree murder, he discovered he had a unique status in this prison. At the bottom were the child molesters, especially the ones who were into boys. There was no real top, but first-degree murder put him in a bubble—behind which he was either feared or ignored—he knew not which. Besides, when things ever got rough, which had happened a few times, he'd bought his way out with boxes of Marlboros. He'd never yet had to resort to a fight.

But he sensed something very bad about this new inmate. Everyone here was awaiting trial. Everyone here was under indictment. So everyone here was "innocent" until . . . But everyone here had been denied bail, ostensibly because they were high risks to disappear, but mostly because they were thought to pose great dangers to society. He looked again at the new one. Yes, he sensed something bad—very bad.

The newcomer turned to him. "I'm Rondo, my friends call me Cola."

"Hey, Cola."

"I didn't say *you* was a friend."

"Whatever you want. I'm Tony."

"I know. They say you the one who shot the family and then fucked the little girl after her brains spilled all over the toilet bowl."

This was bad. He didn't know that this strange rumor had made its way around the outside. He knew a newspaper had initially reported that the police were investigating sexual abuse. When they turned up nothing, he thought he'd heard the end of it. He'd never been charged with that.

"I'm in for murder, nothing else."

"Naw, man, naw. They say you shot the family, shot the little girl right between the eyes, watched her bleed all over the motherfuckin' tiles and then did all that fucking. They say you did it, man."

"They made it up. I'm in for murder."

"You shot the fuckers, yeah?"

Despite every lawyer's admonition, it was considered bad prison code to maintain your innocence to fellow prisoners. How ludicrous, he thought, that he had to consent to being a murderer to appease Cola, yet to deny being a rapist for the same reason. Tony knew that if he said he'd done something sexual to the little girl he'd be fair game for all sorts of prison cruelty. So he strived desperately to hold onto his image—as murderer, non-rapist.

He nodded.

"They say you fucked the little girl."

"I told you I didn't."

"They say you fucked her."

"I didn't."

"Why should I believe you, baby-fucker?"

Tony decided to turn the tables. "What are you in for, Cola?"

Cola jerked his head, surprised at the question. Now he would have to give up his own rank. "What you think, baby-fucking whitey? What you think I'm in for?"

"I think you held up a convenience store and didn't even have the balls to blow away the clerk."

Cola whistled. "Well, whitey's got some mouth on him, doesn't he. Whitey knows the score all right. You pretty bold, whitey." Then Cola wheezed, "And I hear you got yourself one crackpot lawyer. A fruitcake who's gonna waltz you right down to the electric chair. You gonna get fucked to the wall."

"What do you know about my lawyer?"

"All I know is that rich whiteys get rich white lawyers. Poor-ass whiteys like yourself get fruitcakes like us niggers get. And let me tell you, man. Barolo is one super fruit. You gonna know the score by the time he hangs you. You think you know the score now, but you'll know it real good when he hangs you."

"What do you know about Barolo?"

"I know he's fat. I know he's a fat cat. I know he wears fancy-ass watches, silk suits, struts around like the king of the dagos himself, tells lies—big lies that jump out of his hands like jack-in-the-box."

"*How* do you know him?"

"Oh, he batted for me once, whitey. He went to bat, that is. But the wop struck out. He said my case was simple. Like a smooth sell. He said, Cola my man, you and I will fly like birds together—you and I will go to the moon and back. He called it making *love* to the jury. He said, Cola my man, I make love to the jury. I *fuck* the jury, he said. He told me that the jury kisses his feet when he walks into the room, that the jury just loves his big fat watch and his big fat words.

"And then you know what happened, whitey? That jury came back with a big fat verdict—fatter than fat. I got six years just for a small-ass mugging. Six years. Now I'm back. But I'm not counting on Barolo. Naw, man. I'll leave the king of the dagos to you."

24

The Crackerbox was a nothing place. And like all nothing places, it had its appeal. Dark and out of the way, a
small candy shop that no one ever bothered with anymore,
it was a good place for a tryst.

As soon as the pizza place around the corner on Union
Street got video games, the Crackerbox was forgotten.
They were still good for nickel candies and soda and cigarettes for kids who could pass for old enough. But no one
hung out there anymore. And the small lot in back, where
everyone used to skateboard and listen to music, was always
quiet these days.

In the lot, on top of the Dumpster, Tony waited.

He imagined every possible scenario for the visit:
Patricia walking up to him in jeans and a T-shirt. She
would arrive tentatively, cautiously. She would spy him up
on the Dumpster and then come over slowly, with her arms
shyly crossed and her eyes cast downward. Then she would

hop up on the Dumpster next to him and produce a present from behind her back. It would be small, elegantly wrapped, with a dainty red bow. He would unwrap it, with the solemnity and adult patience that he had cultivated for the moment, making sure to preserve the wrapping paper for safekeeping. Inside would be a small framed photograph—the size of a locket—of her. He would take it out, admire it, touch it. Patricia would take his hand in hers, lead him down from the Dumpster, out into the streets of Glen River, where the traffic would stop just for them.

Or perhaps Patricia would come crying, full of teenage grief, so vulnerable in her yellow June sundress and broken heart. She would see him, her kind, noble adolescent savior, sitting atop the Crackerbox Dumpster. She would run to his arms, and he would comfort her. He felt confident he could comfort her. All he needed was the opportunity. How marvelous it would be to hold her against his chest! To massage away the tears and hold her desperation close to his—even if the one did not match the other. He imagined the sensation—the swollen heartbeats, the shallow breaths. If only he could hold her!

He tried to imagine how her small shoulders would feel in his clasp. Never had he held any girl, let alone Patricia, and he knew not how it would feel. His only clues came from hugging his aunt, with her scoliotic spine, thick shoulders, and sickly perfume. He'd always flinched at that. But to hold Patricia would be like holding not the world, but its essence. He knew, at least, that everything worth holding would be contained in her. Like a black hole that contains the density of all matter, so would her soul contain all things. Suddenly it occurred to him that, yes, he would be content to die after holding Patricia once. He tried to understand how it could come to pass that any one girl could contain all things. How could one soul, one body, one mind be the be-all and end-all of worldly experience? For although he knew in his heart that Patricia was the sum total of everything, he didn't know logically how that could be.

Or maybe she would come in humble supplication, asking for Tony's forgiveness, ashamed that she had ever chosen another. She would rest her head in his lap and moan softly. He would be kind but stern and demand her eternal vow that she would never make the same mistake again. She would beg him to accept the promise, which he would each time brush off with a comment like, "You don't mean it." And Patricia would raise her head, hair tousled in the tangle of her young, fledgling emotion: "But I do."

What if she arrived tempered like steel, hardened by loss and resolved to never love another? Then she would renounce romance, ridicule his earnestness, his devotion, his sincere yearnings. She would spare none of his weaknesses, indulge none of his insecurities, administer to none of his wounds. This possibility worried him. After all, she was the experienced one. She'd loved and lost. She'd taken life's chances. By now nothing could blunt her cynical edge. That was the price of getting involved with a sophisticated woman, he told himself. But still it worried him. What could he possibly offer to a woman of the world? What could he offer to a woman who'd lost faith in love when he was just about to celebrate that very faith?

Then a more horrible possibility occurred to him—a nightmare. That Patricia would arrive with Koosh at her side, a reunited couple. If that happened, the pounding he would surely endure at the hands of Koosh would be a comfort compared to the humiliation of the encounter. He would beg to be bludgeoned to death rather than live with the knowledge that Patricia had once again betrayed him—and this time with full knowledge of his plight. He tried to prepare himself for the possibility, though he tried to persuade himself that such a fear was merely that—a fear that existed only on the periphery of nightmare.

Or imagine a dream: Patricia arriving on a horse-drawn carriage—a figment of his fantasies! They would ride off together in mythical splendor, to a land far from Glen River, where no one named Koosh and, in fact, no one else existed. He'd often felt that the only relationship between them would be one where there'd be no other human to interfere—no alcoholic fathers, tyrannical teachers, or superfluous bystanders. If it were only them! If only! He tried to picture it—of course, a tropical island came to mind. The two of them drinking from coconuts, lounging in the breezes, swaying to the lazy melody of a calypso love song. Or it might as well be Alaska. What difference did it make as long as they were alone? He pictured an igloo battered by snow and hail. Not a human in sight. Only a polar bear to keep guard and a fire to warm themselves by.

The image of the igloo drifted into the image of a Glen

River evening as the sun flattened out and the lot behind the Crackerbox slid into shade. Tony sat alone on the Dumpster and watched it happen. For amidst all that fantasizing, all that expectation, all that attempt to picture how she would arrive and on what terms, it had never occurred to him that she wouldn't arrive at all. So he sat and waited. He knew at that point he wasn't waiting for anything except the dark. But that evening he waited for the dark as one might wait for a best friend.

25

"You like jokes?"

"Of course, I like jokes."

Tony lit his first cigarette. He counted six or seven during an average meeting with Barolo.

"All right. Same story. Different ending. Same characters even. But let me start off with a joke."

"Why a joke?"

"I always give the jury a joke. They like jokes. Everyone likes jokes. It's so fucking easy to get away with until the pansy prosecutor objects. Then I just show him up with the punch line. He always feels like an asshole." Barolo leaned over and lowered his voice. "You see, I'm funny. The prosecutor's not. I laugh, he doesn't. I entertain, he doesn't. I'm a man, he's not. I'm not a pansy, he is. It all adds up in the courtroom."

"What kinds of jokes do you tell?"

"Whatever. Sometimes a dirty joke. Sometimes a racist

joke. Maybe a Puerto Rican joke here, an Irish joke there. White, Christ-loving jury: I tell a Jew or black joke. Male jury: I tell a cunt joke. Black jury: I tell a white joke. It's not hard to figure. The prosecutor always objects, it gets stricken from the record, I get balled by the judge—but nine times out of ten I get the joke out, and the jury loves it. And then they say to themselves, *That Barolo he's our man, he's one of us.* He hates kikes as much as we do, or he hates niggers like the best of us.

"I'll put it to you this way, Tony. Who do you believe more: some pansy prosecuting faggot who pulls his socks too high and never smiles, or someone who thinks like you do? You believe in people who are you. I become the jury."

"Where's the joke?"

"Oh yeah, the joke. It's a lawyer joke. I love telling lawyer jokes, 'cause with a lawyer joke you let them know you hate lawyers as much as they do. And all juries hate lawyers. That's the first thing you have to learn as a lawyer. All juries go into a courtroom hating *all* fucking lawyers. But they'll come out loving *one* and hating the *other* enough for the two of them. So this is a lawyer joke. OK.

"The Pope dies and goes to heaven. He gets to St. Peter's gates and, of course, he's expecting a grand fucking reception—champagne, red carpets, the works. Anyway, St. Peter says, *Hold it, Pope, be with you in a minute.* Then St. Peter runs off to greet this other guy the Pope's never seen before. The saint gives this goon royal treatment, puts him in a robe, ushers him to a big white limousine, drives him up to a fabulous mansion with dancing girls, waterfalls, and Dom Perignon on ice. Finally, St. Peter gets back, brings the Pope over to a dirty one-bedroom studio, gives him a glass of tap water and tells the Pope to enjoy himself. So just then, as St. Peter's ready to skedaddle, the Pope turns and says, *Wait a second, St. Peter. What the hell is this. This jackass who I've never seen before comes up here and gets a fucking mansion while I, the Pope, the Holy See himself, arrive at my final resting place and get a lousy studio apartment. So St. Peter leans over and says, *Well, Pope, we've got plenty of you guys up here, but this is our first lawyer."*

"That's funny."

Barolo was still chuckling to himself. "Of course, it's funny. And it works wonders on a fucking jury. All juries know that lawyers are crooks, so you have to show them that you *know* that they know. That's the ticket that most of these losers miss.

"Most lawyers, they try to convince the jury that they're as white and pure as upstate snow. Any jury knows that guy's been pissed on and shit on like any other patch, so they immediately don't trust the guy. His fight's uphill after that. They write him off. What could be worse? You can't *convince* juries of anything. You *seduce* them.

"Let me put it to you this way, Tony. You go to a bar, you meet some chick. You bring her home. She's sitting on your couch. She looks gorgeous. She's got long blond hair, come-get-me eyes. Now one question: What do you do? Do you *ask* her to sleep with you. No, that's for losers. Do you *tell* her to sleep with you. No, that's called rape. Do you *convince* her to sleep with you. No, that won't work. So what the fuck do you do?" Barolo waved his hand. "No, don't answer that. I'll tell you what you do. You *seduce* her. You seduce women, you don't convince them. You make them feel it's their decision. That's the thing about seduction. You don't press down." Barolo offered his thick palm and rotated it upwards, slowly. "You press up—*from within.* That's the beauty of it.

"And with a jury. Well, it's the same fucking thing. You seduce them. You press up from within. If you press down, they sense it and they run over to the prosecutor with their fingers wagging."

"And the story?" asked Tony.

"Yeah, the story. Here it is, story option two. This is the darker side. We start off the same way, so I won't do the whole thing. Young woman meets rich guy, gets big house, kids, all that. I don't have to go over that part again for you, do I?"

"No. I know it well."

Barolo smiled. "So let me start off with this part: the lover, the back-door man. The young, poor guy who's madly in love with Patricia Carver. In fact, so in love he can't think straight. He's loved her for years. He loved her in grade school, he loved her in high school, he loves her in the grave. Maybe we should say, *obsession.* What do you think, Tony? Obsession sound like the right word?"

"It's your story."

"Right, I forgot. I could have sworn someone else scripted it, it rings so damn true. So anyway, we're talking obsession, like I say. This guy follows her everywhere. Then he really gets obsessed. Watches her get married, collects newspaper clippings about her social flutterings, plasters his room with them.

"He goes to his job at the restaurant every day in a daze, 'cause he's always thinking about Patricia. They order halibut, he writes down her name on his order pad. They ask for a napkin, he thinks of the time he got to wipe her face with one. They order a martini, he remembers that's her favorite drink. Whatever they ask for, he serves up Patricia. He lives her, he breathes her. They stiff him on the tip, he doesn't give a shit, 'cause he's thinking Patricia.

"It goes on like this too long. He's tired of being on the outside. He can't take that anymore. So he makes a decision. He's gonna tell Patricia that they're running away together. He has a plan—an escape route of a sort. But let me get to the night.

"So it's a drizzly, kind of chilly night. The type that murder-mystery writers like. The kind of night where the bones don't fit together in the sockets too well. So our spurned lover arrives at the seafood dive for his shift, and right away he makes a decision. He's got his gun in his gym bag, in the locker, so how hard would it be, he thinks. Besides, he's not really thinking, he's moving in a daze. His tables clear out a little early, so he sneaks out early. He's not really supposed to cut out. After all, he's got all that cleaning up stuff to do and tables to set, but he's impatient—he's itching for action, for *something*. For anything, but just an end to the not knowing, to the unhappiness, to the fucking desperation.

"So he cuts out early. He gets in his car and without

thinking about it, he starts out toward Hautucket Bay, toward the Hollow. The trees are full of demons. It's a short trip at that hour but it seems to never end. He winds his way down those rich, quiet roads. No cars. No people. Just the night. He knows the way well by now. These roads—these confusing, rainy, unmarked roads that just roll on and on—he knows as well as he knows the moles on Patricia's hand.

"And then he arrives. He parks at the base of the drive—that long gravel driveway that goes all the fucking way up—the one the newspapers would love to snap photos of later. He parks his car in the grove where he usually does, off to the left, where no one will notice. Then he climbs on foot. He's happy with himself 'cause he's made his decision. He looks down at his gloved hand: he's holding a gun. It's a big gun—twice the size of his cock, in fact. Which is good 'cause it's gonna have to do what his cock couldn't: conquer Patricia.

"At the top of the hill, he pauses to look at the big house. He'd never noticed before how pretty it was there at night, with the sound of the bay in the background. He gets closer. He studies the house. It's lights out in the kiddies' rooms. The light's on in Kirk Carver's study and in one of the bathrooms. Everyone accounted for—except the one he's come for.

"He walks around the side, pretty sure that no one can make him out in that soupy night. And he sees her. There she is in the kitchen, fussing around like a typical suburban wife. She's opening the fridge, she's putting something in the fucking microwave. She looks content, oblivious. He hates that look. But he looks closely anyway. You know, one last look . . .

"He crouches in the shrubs, takes out a wire cutter, snips the phone lines and disables the alarm. Then he checks his pocket for the lock pick. He loads the big gun and prepares himself. He says a prayer. After all, we're talking about a future minister here. Then he walks back around to the front of the house and lets himself in the front door.

"Everything's quiet in the big house. He breathes in the smells of Carver money: new upholstery, fancy perfume, rich leather. To him, it all has the stench of death. He takes off his shoes and starts to climb the creaky wooden stairs, two at a fucking time. He goes right to the old codger's study at the end of the hall. He looks in and sees Carver reading. He walks up quietly, puts the gun to the temple and pulls the trigger almost before the poor fucker even gets a chance to look up.

"Then he hears screams. He has to hurry. He runs down the hall—to the bathroom. He opens the door, sees Melody on the can. He pops her in the head before she even has a chance to pull up her undies.

"Then it's off to little Teddy's room. This two-year-old is still asleep, dreaming of fairy land and his mommy. He never wakes up—that's just as well. He gets to die peacefully.

"Finally, our killer runs downstairs. He traps Patricia just as she's trying to run out of the kitchen to get out of the house. Of course, she wasted a big second picking up the phone receiver to call the police. Once she found the line dead, she ran for the door. But there he was, with a gun. She begs for mercy. He says, *Fuck you.*

"Well, how does that sound, Tony? Does that sound like a realistic story to you?"

"What if I say I think you left out a few things."

"Oh yeah?" asked Barolo, genuinely curious, adjusting and readjusting his watchband. "What if you do say so? Does that mean it's a true story?"

Tony looked at the cold steel behind Barolo and the clock on the wall. The guard would be coming any minute. "Like you like to say, Mr. Barolo, there's no such thing as truth. Only stories, good and bad."

26

When nine years pass in a place like Glen River, it means very little, really. No coups d'état. No new civilizations. No great discoveries. No proclamations nailed to the church door. No visits from the President. No cataclysms. Nothing of biblical proportions. But, then again, nine is not a biblical number—like seven, for example.

But of course there are changes: A new McDonald's on Firth Street. A business fallen into bankruptcy. A few fewer jobs. A higher property tax. Another mall or two. VCRs now in every home. A fresh paint job on the municipal pool.

Then there are the personal changes, and these are many. New babies born. New gravestones in the cemetery. A few couples tying the knot. A few more unraveling it. A confirmation here, an anniversary there. This house reapplianced the kitchen, that house retiled the bathroom. Small milestones, maybe. But no less important than anything else.

If you looked deeper, would you see more than you would at first glance? Would you see a new way of life or a new philosophy? No, probably not. But evolution—or de-volution—is a slow process and if you'd been around at the time of Cro-Magnon man, you wouldn't have made out the small changes then either: A back ever so slightly un-hunching itself over the centuries; strands of hair receding from the palm at the rate of six per decade; a forehead be-coming civilized and less protruding over the course of thousands of years; the opposable thumb redefining itself. No, nine is a tiny number overall—and still pretty small in the aging of a community—but in one person's life it looms large.

He waited by the street corner. Down the way, twenty feet, was the auto showroom. A couple arrived, squeaky clean, reasonably dressed, smiles all around. They were the type to buy a car, he thought. They looked eager, im-pressionable, ready to be fleeced. God, he realized, he could have been good at this business if he'd ever gotten a foot in. It seemed so easy to sell. He could smell suck-ers so quickly.

They shook hands with the young saleswoman. She stood tall, elegantly appointed, not a typical Islander in the clothes or hair—too sophisticated—clearly North Shore. She was dressed way beyond her means, even if she was on the top of the charts for commissions that month.

He watched her gesticulate, talk, wave her hand toward the new blue sedan, showily indicate the green coupe. She was good at what she did, he thought. But how could it have been otherwise. She'd always been good at what she did. Or at least it had seemed so to him.

He didn't know how long to watch. He could've stood there all day. Once you've been away for so long, it doesn't seem to matter how long you watch or stay. But he figured he'd stay awhile. And he felt as though he'd spent his whole life watching, and in some ways he had.

It struck him as important that she was so very much the same. Even as a woman, she hadn't lost that way of tossing her hair to one side with an impatience that had always seemed to say she was bigger than her place in life— bigger than anything surrounding her. She still had the same creamy skin: perfect, he could see through the glass. Never had she had a blemish and never would she. Though now walled up in glass and steel, she was the same beachcomber—and he the same misplaced spectator looking in.

He had thought that the years spent traveling, surrounded by new customs, new people, in and out of brothels and rooming houses, he would've forgotten. He'd counted on forgetting. But with each new woman, with each new job, his memory had only sharpened, and his grip on his surroundings had only loosened. Stranger than the force of memory was its method. It would come to him incoherently, in fits and starts, without faces or names. Only feelings. But sometimes these feelings, the longing and the hopelessness were so strong and ill-defined that he would shiver in fear and sweat, and wait miserably for dawn.

There were places he'd visit in dreams, unknown places that only seemed familiar in their loneliness and their desolation. Faces were the same way, and he learned to recognize strangers in his dreams.

And then there was always Patricia.

When he was spent and exhausted in bed, finally drifting off, done with the ravages of the manic tossing and turning, he would turn to the wall and see her. He would view her as a childhood illusion, preserved as an icon, and like an icon always gleaming with an importance beyond itself.

Now he could see her again in the flesh.

Patricia took the couple over to the desk and they passed papers back and forth. *Congratulations*, he heard himself say under his breath. They'd decided to sign. He watched the small, bald man with nervous mannerisms and an obsequious smile lift the pen and then pause to glance at his wife. She nodded and he drew his hand across the page. Then there were more papers and more signings and hurried smiles and handshakes.

Patricia escorted her customers across the showroom floor and handed them over to another sales rep who lacked similar charm and style—on whom a smile, Tony noticed, seemed only affected decorum and politeness.

He watched her as she returned to her desk, fiddled with some belongings in the drawer and then sat down to complete more paperwork. If she'd turned just then, she would have seen him through the same lens he saw her: the disparate changes that melt to nothingness in the familiarity of a gaze, a hand movement, a grimace. She wouldn't have been able to see the weariness of the years or the wiliness garnered from drifting about after dropping out of school.

He saw his own reflection in the showroom window. It was superimposed on Patricia sitting behind the desk. For the first time ever he saw their two images side by side, as if in a tender snapshot taken of two lovers. Except that in this image, one figure had no interaction with the other. One watched and the other worked, oblivious to the presence of the one. The images were incongruous. It reminded him of some sort of double exposure—a pure accident— a photographer's mistake.

He'd had a girlfriend in Santa Fe who'd reminded him of Patricia. Of course, every girlfriend had reminded him in some way—sometimes the smallest of ways—like this Latino girl who'd worn her hair in braids and looked nothing like Patricia, yet tipped her head so similarly: at the same angle, with the same lilt to it, with the same flash of irreverence. He'd met her at the Albuquerque bus station and shared a Coors with her. Then they'd walked over to a nearby trailer park and found an empty camper and broken in. He'd been struck by that trailer park on the fringe of the great adobe landscape. Little metal houses overlooking the desert—like lemmings on the precipice of the sea, he'd thought.

They'd spent three days there, drinking, fucking, and listening to the little portable radio that could get stations from Taos, Phoenix and Las Vegas all at once. Then the owners returned and they had to flee north into the Sandia Mountains. There, in that bewildering landscape that changed hues with his emotions, Tony got tired of his new girlfriend. She no longer reminded him of Patricia. Instead, she reminded him only of what she was not. Her kindness, her warmth, the way she slid her tongue down his throat until it made his own as dry as sawdust—these were not traits of his beachcomber, and he became discouraged.

On the way to Santa Fe, they visited an Indian pueblo, and he lost her there, among the tunnels and ladders of that ancient city. He never thought of her again, except once, when a state trooper questioned him about a young Latino girl who'd been missing from her family for days and had last been seen heading north, for the mountains. Tony fit the description of the guy she'd last been seen with, the trooper said. He'd left New Mexico the next day. After that he never thought of her again. It never occurred to him.

Tony watched Patricia leave the showroom through the big glass double doors and wave a few good-byes to the other salesmen who, with their come-ons and crude jokes, showed none of the proper signs of deference to a woman who was way out of their league.

She climbed into a red Ferrari Testarossa. He thought he recalled her once saying that that was her dream car. He crossed the street and got into his old Buick, swung into a U-turn and pulled out onto Northern Boulevard two cars behind her. It was a nice day, and she had the top down and the radio on. What a thing, he thought, to be such a beautiful girl and ride through Long Island in a red sports car with the radio on. That was it: that was the meaning of life, right there, contained in that small box of automation.

He took a left with her onto Harbor Cote Drive. Though he was directly behind her now, and though she showed no sign of taking any notice of the old dusty boat behind her that had been following her for over six miles, he allowed another car to slip between them as a precaution.

He recalled living in Providence, where he'd gotten a job as a cab driver at the age of seventeen. When business was slow and there were no fares, he'd pick a car driven by the most beautiful woman he could find and follow her relentlessly. At first he'd been unskilled and lost his targets many times, either in traffic or at a light, or by following so closely that he would arouse their suspicions to the point where he had to turn away. But after a while he perfected his technique, learning how to follow in their blind spots, to the left and behind, and time the yellow lights perfectly. At the height of his skill, he would follow cars all the way out to the suburbs, turning off only after he'd watched his target pull into her home's driveway. Eventually, he'd been fired for ignoring the dispatcher.

But now that he was following the one that he'd always wanted to be following, always had imagined himself to be following, he felt empty. Just like with the Providence women that he'd followed home to their husbands and children and secure garages, he knew this would end the same way—with him on the outside staring in.

Tony turned right and watched her ease the Ferrari onto Cove Road and then speed past the sign that read *Entering Hautucket Bay—Private Community—Not a Through Way.* He slowed down as she did as they passed the lush foliage on either side that marked the beginning of the big estates. Then he watched her turn off into a gated drive where the grille doors swung open as she entered. He sped past and glimpsed the name on the elegant filigree signpost:

CARVER

Nine years later, only the names had changed.

27

Tony always walked out of the room with Barolo the way people walk out of weddings these days: with the knowledge that there's a better than fifty-fifty chance it's all a big mistake. But he liked Barolo, liked talking to him, so he didn't mind so much. Either Barolo would spring him or he wouldn't. And either way Tony would have the same small life in the end.

Today after he walked out of the room, mail call found him a letter from Charlotte. It was in a tiny envelope this time—as though, since the last letter went unanswered, this one would be more modest in appearance. But the size of the envelope was deceptive, because the letter was written on very thin onion paper—several sheets—that had been folded into a wad and stuffed into a diminutive envelope. Tony counted the pages: five.

He resisted reading it at first. The last letter, the last betrayal, still pained him. Yet, a desire to know how she'd taken his silence beckoned to him to flatten the pages and begin reading. Yet, other thoughts surfaced to stop him. How could he forgive her treachery? How could he want to speak to this woman who had courted him by mail only to inform him that she was seeing someone on the side? Even as a minister he hadn't found it in his heart to forgive, so how could he do so as a spurned mate? Ludicrous, he decided, to forgive anyone, ever, for anything. Even if it went against all the teachings of the church to say so.

But the letter did call to him, with its petite physique and its sensuous folds. And there were what looked like many, many words there. Maybe it was unfair not to give such a letter a chance. Maybe there was just too much curiosity in him to let it go.

There was no exotic perfume scent this time. He spun the envelope around. No waxy kisses. A bland envelope, bare except for its barest essentials: a stamp, an address and a return address.

These were worrisome omens. To withhold a kiss is serious business. To forsake the perfume seemed utterly unforgivable—so cruel an act to a man who can only smell prison smells like the hybrid disinfectants of his cell or the metallic, washed-out odor of jailhouse dinner. Revenge. Revenge for his not having written back. Now he had to read the letter, if only to discover how she explained herself.

He tortured himself by allowing his imagination to consider what a life with Charlotte could be like. Actually, he'd practiced this self-deception several times. He pictured the vindication at trial, Barolo's hearty embrace, the release through the courthouse doors, Charlotte smiling on the steps, the real live feel of real live lips, hopping into a car— wedding day and release day all wrapped in one. The American Dream: freedom and a family. Like that. He snapped his fingers.

But then again, he had never believed in dreams, America, or the American Dream. To Tony, they were all the type of farce that made even the actors laugh out loud inopportunely. What was the point of dreams when you were only destined to awake from them, destined to interpret them, destined to be deceived by them? He had once read that time follows a different sequence in dreams—a sequence that is fractured, nonsensical, irrelevant to real life. Time cannot be grasped in dreams. Proportion becomes skewed and expanded so that a minute becomes a day, a day a month, a month a year. He had experienced that phenomenon as sure as anyone who dreams of a lifetime of experiences and then awakens to find they've napped for ten minutes. So it struck him as odd that any prisoner would dare to dream. Anyone who was doing hard time would surely be crazy to expand a minute ever so dramatically as that. If he could find a way of doing the opposite—of compressing time so that a year of real time could be traversed in a second through the trick of imagination, then dreams might become worthwhile.

As it was, dreams made him ill.

He flattened out the thin papers and began to read:

Dear Inmate #90245,

Tony.

Since you didn't write back last time, I figured you wouldn't want another letter from me but I couldn't resist. I had to explain myself but I'm almost scared to even try it. I know you were hurt by the stuff I told you last time, but you have to remember that I'm trying my best and I'm trying to get out of this bad relationship the same way you're trying to get out of jail. It's the same kind of thing. We're both in these places through no fault of our own. I guess that's just the way the world works. I told my sister about you. She says I'm nuts to be writing you letters. She calls you a psycho murderer and says that when you get out of jail the first thing you'll do is kill me. I know she's wrong and I tell her so every time we talk about it. I showed her the letters you'd written me. She thought they were weird so it didn't help things much. But my sister's the type who would never understand something like this. She's got a normal life with a husband and kids and she doesn't understand people that've had the world turn upside down for them like you and me. . . .

Tony stopped reading and looked up at the bars in front of him. He thought of the phrase, *that've had the world turn upside down for them.* He repeated it aloud: *that've had the world turn upside down for them.*

It struck him as an overly exotic and poetic expression for what was the most prosaic and banal truth—that the world had disappointed them as it had disappointed so many countless others.

. . . But when I think of the happiness that we could have to-
gether, when I think of these things it gives me some kind of
hope—sometimes just the smallest bit. I find myself knowing that
you understand things the same kind of way I do. I'm ready to
leave him. I really am. I picture us in a nice big house. The kind
you read about. I want all the things I've never had . . .

Tony put aside the letter. It was really a form letter, he
decided. Like any form letter, not addressed to any particular person, only to an idea of a person. Not that such a
thought discouraged him. For, as he slid onto his bunk and
threw off his prison-issue shoes, it occurred to him that all
letters are form letters. Every letter, though addressed as it
might be to Aunt Marie, Cousin Billy, Lover Cindy, Friend
Max, was targeted at something that didn't really exist—
the poor misguided shadow of the conception that the ad-
dressee was a confidant, a soulmate, an alter ego—the one.
And every letter was a lie, wrapping the sender in robes of
fiction.

He composed the letter he would like to write to
Charlotte in his mind—what he would write if he could
break past the form letter and the harness of convention
that constrained him and hid his true self:

Dear Charlotte,

I will never send this letter because I can't. It tells you of things
I don't dare tell. It tells the true story of who I am and what I've
done. I live with that knowledge. It's about time . . .

Then came the harsh buzzer that marked a headcount, and the guards started down the corridor. Tony moved to the front of his cell to present himself. That mental epistle— that letter of disclosure, of honesty, of freedom—dissolved as suddenly, and was forgotten. It would have to wait, like so many things, for another day.

28

As everyone knows, there are several traditions more American than apple pie. There's tax evasion, of course. Everyone acknowledges that. And then motels—who wouldn't add those to the list? And what about shopping malls? A close third? Then there are above-ground pools, tag sales, Jell-O brand gelatin and the whole rest of it.

And somewhere in that random assortment of all things that reside in some or every corner of the fifty states is that living piece of the darker side of Americana: the stalker.

That first day back in Long Island, Tony decided to become a stalker, and made it so. The job requirements were minimal: a target, dubious intentions, and lots of time. He was well equipped.

Of course, as with any job, there are not just requirements but tools. He had those, too: A pair of binoculars, a set of surveillance transmitters, a car, a camera with telephoto lens. He spent a few days preparing this equipment.

Sure, he was familiar with things like this. He was, of course, no newcomer to the ways of watching. But he felt this was the big time: real stalking. He had to be careful.

He decided that stalking, if done right, was akin to marriage or any other version of intimacy. What could speak more of closeness than following and watching someone constantly? What could be more cozy?

He started small—with stunts like following Patricia home from work. Or watching her arrive early in the morning. But soon his ambitions grew. He wanted to track her everywhere. He wanted to install cameras in the big fancy house she often visited at night that had the plaque with the name *Carver* filigreed in front of it. He wanted to photograph her at work, at home, in bed—in other beds.

Finally, when he had established the basic pattern of her days and nights, Tony decided to make his first, bold venture. He parked outside her house—a two-family that had been divided into smaller apartments—on an evening when he knew she was at Carver's. Putting on a black baseball cap and a false mustache, he examined himself in the mirror. He wasn't sure if a disguise was necessary, but he felt the desire to dress up. And now that he'd created a new physical self, he found it gave him a rush.

As he emerged from the car and started across the dark street, he found a growing sense of incompetence clouding his plans. After all, he had only read a small selection of how-to manuals and magazines to understand the process of installing a sound-monitoring device. He had it in hand. It was a small metal cup, of the type that looks like a shrunken satellite dish. He had chosen such a device for the simplicity of setting it up. He hadn't wanted to attempt to break into Patricia's apartment, for he felt that would be too risky. That eliminated all the standard bugging and surveillance devices, most of which needed to be implanted directly into the phone. So he'd found an ad for the *Sniper Window-Mounted Audio Dish* in a spy aficionado magazine and immediately sent off for it. Two weeks after he mailed his money order for $69.95, the device arrived in a small brown box that bore no return address.

The advantage of the Sniper Window-Mounted Audio Dish was that it could be installed on a bracket, at an angle above the window frame, on the outside of the wall. The drawback, of course, was that the unit, though quite small, would be visible from the street. But Tony had carefully chosen a bedroom window in Patricia's apartment that was partially obscured by a great, overhanging oak tree. Not only would he be able to use the tree as a ladder to mount the gadget, but the leaves and branches would obscure the unit's presence—at least until fall.

The instructions claimed that the small dish would pick up any sounds emitted in the room it was targeted on and transmit them as far as 5,000 yards to a base receiver. This part could be plugged into a car's cigarette lighter and monitored while driving.

Tony had never bothered to determine whether his surveillance activity was a felony, nor had he bothered to figure out if the unit could really transmit with the quality that had been claimed. But there he was anyway, with a cap and a fake mustache, excited by the possibilities.

But he couldn't shake the cloud of incompetence as he crossed the street or even while standing in the very shadows of the massive tree he would soon set about climbing. He had never had much faith in his ability to execute technical tasks, and they always seemed all the harder when there was a woman involved. He inspected the items in his backpack before climbing: one penlight (which he imagined he would hold in his mouth once he was in position), one Sniper Window-Mounted Audio Dish, one manual wood drill (the kind the phone company technician uses), many screws and brackets for mounting, and one big screwdriver.

He realized that by installing a permanent earpiece in Patricia's apartment, he would possess her in a way that previously would have been inconceivable. To own her phone conversations, her sighs, her cries, and her laughter—these were things he'd often dreamed of collecting. He imagined a whole library of audio tapes—with an index and a concordance he would publish of every possible expression, every probable exhalation.

His hands shook with excitement as he allowed himself to imagine this scenario. He fumbled with the tools and the screwdriver fell to the ground. He had to climb down and start up again. This time he approached the task with the type of concentration he could only muster by working in the minutiae of his project—by drilling the holes with microscopic precision, by turning the screws with absolute focus. His brow creased. Sweat beaded. Finally, he was done.

Now it was time to get back in the car and test the receiver. Before descending, he activated the dish by installing a small battery and making sure that the angle was properly fixed on the window pane. The blind had been drawn so that he couldn't get a view of the bedroom. But, from this exact perch, he had viewed the contents of it once before: the luxurious goosedown comforter, the bed with elegant brass fixtures, the dresser with photos he hadn't been able to make out, the absence of any small personal items.

On his way down, he scanned nervously for witnesses, but the only sound was his own awkward scampering and the heaviness of his breathing. Back in his car he flicked the button on the receiver and watched the power light glow in the half-darkness. First there was static, then a fuzzy quiet once the receiver honed in on its transmitter. It was the proverbial sound of silence—the low, inconsequential, grasping hum of a house when no one's home.

He fell asleep there, in the pleasant womb of the silence of the bedroom that played itself fifty yards away in the car.

Until she came home.

She must have parked on the other side, because he hadn't heard the car pull up. But all of a sudden, the loud noise of a door slamming awakened him and he realized that it was her. The sounds over the receiver electrified the dark: there was the sound of the door and then of footsteps with high heels, then of a refrigerator door opening and closing, of the water tap turned on, of the toilet flushing. He was thrilled by the sensations and the sounds, by the overlap of her space into his. He was living her life now with her.

And then the footsteps were louder. She was entering the bedroom. He heard the bedsprings heave, then the covers rustling. But these sounds were barely perceptible, like half-whispers. He had to cock his ear and hold his breath.

Then the beeps of a touch-tone phone being dialed. Then half of a dialogue which he would never forget.

Hello.
Pause.

I'm here.
Pause.

Of course, baby, I will.
Pause.

Don't worry. I love you.
Pause.

I love you.
Pause.

G'night.
Pause.

Hmmm.

And then the sound of the receiver clattering into its cradle. And then the sound once more of bedsheets rustling. And then the sound of breathing. And that was all.

Breathing.

A monotony that wouldn't cease until dawn.

He was as if next to her, but not. And the torture of it felt like a punishment he deserved. What had he done but learn she would never, ever breathe beside him in the flesh. He drove home, more alone than he'd ever been, clicking the receiver off as soon as he hit the first traffic light.

29

In trials, as in all things, never say *never*.

So said Barolo to Tony on the day before opening arguments:

"Never say *never*. What the fuck do you want from me? You pin me down and ask me if I said I *never* lost a case. I never fucking said *never*. That would be unlike me, 'cause I don't use those tight-ass words, if you know what I mean. I don't believe in that sort of pronouncement. 'Cause you don't know what they throw you till you get in the ring. And nothing ever goes the way you want it to.

"Not that I think we have any chance of losing. I mean I've got the prosecutor shitting in his pants. The young *assistant* prosecutor.

"And Judge Kirschner. That's all worked out. Judge Kirschner is an old friend. We went to law school together—a few years apart—but he knows me. He knows my stuff. He's been there for the Barolo punch a time or two. He's a Jewish judge. They're easy on criminals. They love to bend over backwards for the sake of your cocka-mamie civil liberties. So don't worry a bit. And if it comes down to it, I just tell the judge what I know about him. 'Cause I tell you, it ain't too pretty. And if it comes to it, I tell him what I know.

"I don't give a fuck about rules. That's for the little guy—the crackpots—the weirdos. This prosecutor calls me six times a day threatening me with this and that rule. He files every fucking motion there is. He doesn't even have any evidence, so he tries to block all of mine. Can you fucking believe it? No state's evidence! It's an embarrass-ment!

"The pansy was relying on the maid's testimony. Turns out she's lying, saying she saw you sneaking around to save Carver's honor. I'm gonna impeach her, Tony. She's out. How? Carver gives her twenty grand right before this came down to keep his family life quiet. I trace that from bank account to bank account. Sure enough it has Carver writ-ten all over it. It *smells* Carver. So she's out. State can't have her. State can't have anything I don't want it to have. That's the way I work, Tony. State takes orders from me.

"Reminds me of a client I once had that had his wife knocked off. He had a wall of witnesses lined up against him: the postman who heard screams, the little honey he'd been screwing who turned against him, the insurance agent he'd called to change the policy a week before—I mean this guy was not looking at an easy case, and neither was I, I tell you, Tony.

"I walked into the judge's chambers knowing everything. You need to know *everything*. I don't mean knowing the New York statute backwards and forwards. I mean knowing *reality*: like what the judge had for lunch that day, if he's burping up pepperoni or sausage, who he fucked the night before, what his favorite song is, the name of the daughter in the cute photo on his desk, if his son is a second baseman or a pitcher.

"This is the real shit that gives or doesn't give in a case. Forget about all that legal shit you read about. I'm telling you it happens all between you and that judge, and then between you and that jury, but never between you and the law. *Never*.

"It's like this. Let me give you an idea of how it works. I get a client tomorrow who walks into my office with a gunshot wound in his arm, a gun in his hand, hair down to his ass, saying a cop just interrupted him in the act of something—he won't say what—and bloodied him up. Then he holds up the gun and says he's holding a .44 Magnum and he doesn't know how it got there. Then you look at his face and notice it matches up with the photo on the wall of the county's most wanted. Well, what's the most important detail in all that?

"Well, let me tell you. The long hair—the hair that makes him look like Charles Manson before he even walks in the door—and will make him look that way at the hearing. So what do you do? You tell him to put the gun down, cut the hair, shut up, call the police and an ambulance—in that order.

"Little details. Lawyers deal in details. *Big* lawyers deal in little details. Anyone will tell you that. Lawyers measure just how big they are by how little their details are. It's the trade. You can't deal with the big picture until you have the details under your belt. A lawyer tells me he's big, I ask him how small he is.

"People ask me why I defend people like you, Tony, you know, they ask that all the time. Why defend the scumbags, pimps, murderers, and sleazebags, they ask. I always say the same thing. I say: *You are closer to those scumbags than you think you are. You are one step away. With your big house and your lovely wife and your fine kids, you are only one step away.*

"And I mean it. The line is so thin. So thin. I know guys who are one step away all the time. They get up in the morning and it could go either way. Today, with Junior's graduation and Missy's birthday party it goes one way. But tomorrow, with their wife's affair and the stock market crash, it could go the other.

"People are always so close to snapping. So fucking close. That's what gets me. That's what keeps me in this business. I wait for them to snap. Then the same bozo who lectured me about my profession a year ago is crawling to me on his knees because he's facing twenty years. If he doesn't see a shrink first he comes to me. And *I* decide what happened—just like I did with you. *I* decide.

"Sometimes people make that one mistake. It's a real one—a bit fat fuckup. You can tell the one-timers. They break down and cry. They ask for forgiveness. They get sick and vomit on my expensive leather sofa. I pity them. I let them cry. I let them feel sorry for themselves—for about ten minutes. Then I tell them to stop whining and figure a way out. They never can. That's when I step in. And they're grateful. They are truly, truly fucking *grateful.*

"I let them try to figure a way out so they can see how hard it is. Once they appreciate that, they worship me. They know they'd be lost without me. I'm the only hope. I get off on that, I really do.

"When I was young, real young—just turned eleven—everyone came over to my house one day for a birthday party. You know, it was one of those bullshit affairs where your uncle dresses up as a clown for the day and does jokes and a magic act. Well, you would have loved it, Tony, I'll never forget it. It was in our house on Pelham Parkway in the Bronx. Relatives, friends. There was a whole bunch of schoolyard kids, of course, and then the usual neighbors and all that jazz. It was a real Italian thing: lots of calzones and then cannolis for dessert, you know. My mother wasn't the greatest cook, but boy could she load it on. And I was proud that day, Tony. I was just turning eleven. I was a big wheel because most of those loser kids on the block were still ten. This made me the big man: you have to understand the way it worked on Pelham Parkway.

"So when it was time to finally file into our little back-yard there for the magic act, I got excited. But then something happened. My uncle was stomping around cursing that someone had stolen the props for his act. Now I knew that it had to be my cousin Paolo 'cause I'd seen him only three minutes before running down the hall with a smirk on his face as wide as the Brooklyn Bridge.

"And sure enough, I found Paolo in a closet playing with all that shit—the clown mask, the magic hat, the little foam rubber balls and cups for the hide-the-ball trick, even the wand with the red rubber tips. He was just sitting there at the bottom of the fucking closet, playing with that shit like he was the king of the house and no one would ever catch on. I'll never forget how stupid I found that. How stupid could someone be, I thought to myself, to steal all that shit from our crazy uncle who had a temper you did not want to fuck with? How stupid could a little kid be. So I asked him. I asked Paolo how he could be so dumb. I told him to throw the shit as quick as he could into my little brother Benito's room, who was too young to be held responsible.

"So we ran down the hall and dumped all the magic stuff in between Benito's toys. And just in time, too, 'cause a second later our uncle came down the hall cursing and yelling that he was going to find Paolo and beat the shit out of Paolo 'cause he knew Paolo had made off with his stuff. But when I pointed at all his stuff thrown on the floor in Benito's room, he went in there and collected it all. Then he came out into the hall and looked at the two of us. And he told Paolo that he knew he'd thrown the stuff into Benito's room to cover himself. So I said to Uncle, I said, *You know Paolo's not smart enough to think of that.* And Uncle looked back at me and said, *That's true—and you're too smart to think of it,* and winked.

"And Tony, you know what, Uncle was right. I was too smart and Paolo was too stupid. That's the way it was. But I still knew I had to defend him. Because he was too guilty *and* too stupid. I tried my best. It was my first case, and I won—even though the judge knew the whole truth. That's when I learned, Tony, that the truth never gets in the way unless you let it."

30

Life can present no more lonely option than attendance as a guest at your beloved's wedding.

Is there any gathered here among us who feels that this couple should not be so joined by the eternal pledges of marital devotion? If so, let him speak now or forever hold his peace.

But, then again, there are those magic words.

There are so few milestones in life that allow for the option to object. Funerals, birthdays, holidays. All these come and go with a regularity unmatched. There's no way to stop them. Objections hold no sway.

Why then weddings?

For every couple happily wed there's someone sitting somewhere who would love to pull the plug on it. It could be an uncomfortable relation, an outraged father-in-law-to-be, a spiteful friend, a worried grandmother, or just a well-meaning prophet who can see the divorce looming around the corner. Or it could be a jealous outsider—someone who'd prefer to be exchanging vows himself.

Tony sat in the back row of the elegant North Shore Episcopal Church. The benches were wood brown, the walls virgin white, the tuxedoes deathly black. He was thankful for the scale of the proceedings: the large number of guests amassed on either side of the aisle, the huge bouquets of flowers that graced the appropriate places, the well-groomed ushers who rushed to and fro escorting family members. The large scale offered anonymity. Anonymity he needed. For he still wasn't sure if Patricia would recognize his face after all these years. And he didn't want her to have any rude surprises on her wedding day.

Tony tried to remember whether he'd ever been at a wedding before. He thought he must have because the whole set looked familiar. But then he realized that the knowledge could just as easily come from half a dozen movies. A wedding always looked staged anyway. In reality, it always was. The scale of the wedding was big—this was the North Shore—but it was also Episcopal—so everything was muted and refined.

He tried desperately to imagine how Patricia would look coming down the aisle. Kirk Carver was already standing stiffly in front of the minister, waiting to kiss his bride.

He allowed himself to imagine that kiss now, so that he would be prepared for it later. He had to have that preparation for his own sake. So he set about the task of imagining.

But before he had placed those lips together in his mind, the wedding march began and he watched the procession. The beauty of it as a celebration dawned on him in a sudden and shocking way. Never had he seen anything so beautiful in all his life. Never had he seen anything so stunning as this bride. And it was obvious that nearly all the guests shared his sentiments, judging by the palpable rush of breath emitted from so many mouths.

He cowered in the beauty of it. His hands shook. How could he ever have imagined that it would be like this? That this ceremony, one in which he had always fantasized himself a groom rather than an outsider, would be the most fantastic thing he had ever witnessed? He watched in awe as the procession passed his seat.

Though he was witnessing her make that natural conversion, that final maturation from beachcomber to bride, Tony felt that he was still watching a little girl. No doubt Patricia's father who, despite his wide girth and unsteady gait, looked quite distinguished in his silver hair and tuxedo as he prepared to give her away, must have been thinking the same thing. It occurred to Tony that by all rights he should have been Patricia's brother or father, for his emotions were much more suited to the role.

It was life's most lonely option. This was the reality Tony had to face as he watched everything spin perilously closer and closer to that stage where everything becomes knitted with *I do*. As the minister spoke, irreligious desperation possessed Tony—a desire to do anything to stop this madness—to stop the manic crescendo of happiness that seemed to exclude no one else but him. He waited for those words, the words that allowed someone, an unknown party perhaps, to stop the proceedings—to prevent the ceremony from its conclusion. Finally, they came:

Is there any gathered here among us who feels that this couple should not be so joined by the eternal pledges of marital devotion? If so, let him speak now or forever hold his peace.

Then followed the traditional silence that attaches to those words, the heart-stopping moment where everyone waits for a lone voice to find itself in the big hall; for some outside influence to damage the beauty of the proceedings, to tarnish the nuptials that are beyond reproach. Tony sat shivering, knowing that he could say nothing and by doing so had become an accomplice to this affair. The silence lingered, as did his inaction. Finally, the guests breathed out their expectation and the minister concluded the ceremony. A first and final kiss. An eternal embrace.

Tony followed the guests to the reception at the Maidstone Yacht Club. It was a gorgeous, light, breezy June day. It was the kind of day that people like to say would be nice for a wedding.

He wasn't sure why he would attend the reception. On the drive, he joked with himself that it would be rude to leave early. Then he joked that it would be ruder still to attend the reception without bearing a gift. By the time he arrived, his sense of humor had run dry and he stopped joking. He gave his key to the valet and basked briefly in the sun on his way into the club. Adequately dressed in his best suit and wingtip shoes, he nevertheless found it hard to feel inconspicuous, especially without a place setting assigned for him.

On his way to the magnificent waterside patio where the festivities would be held, he paused to get a vodka and tonic at the bar. Then, after the band played some swing and the newlyweds had danced, it was announced that the husband would be giving the first toast. Tony moved to the front rim of guests who had situated themselves at the edge of the dance floor.

Kirk Carver was a handsome man, there was no doubt about it. Tall, almost gangly, but youthful for his age and fit, he lifted his glass and came to the microphone. Behind him, magnificently silhouetting his shoulders, lapped the calm waters of the Sound, now tinted auburn with the lowering arc of the sun.

It couldn't have been a more perfect picture. Sure enough, the wedding photographer was acrobatically dancing this way and that, preparing to capture every angle, every gesture, every platitude.

A man clearly accustomed to being listened to, Kirk Carver only paused and looked out at the guests. There was a sudden deferential, expectant silence. The water lapped, the moment was his:

When I was ten, I made two decisions: that I would become

President of the United States, number one; and two, that I would marry a beautiful woman. Now, one out of two ain't bad at all. My acquaintances always doubted the first ambition, but those who really knew me doubted the second more. They'd ask how a bum like me would ever end up with a wonderful wife. And today they deserve an answer: Friends, I don't know. . . .

There was laughter and applause. And then a silence more profound than before.

But I'm happy to say that it happened, as all of you with or without glasses can clearly see. What you can't as clearly see, though, is just how beautiful Patricia is inside as well as outside. She is the very definition of beauty. Thank heavens I got to see that side before someone else skated off with her. It makes me proud, as I take her as my wife, to know that she is a woman of true character, of devotion, ready to sacrifice, ready to be true to me and to our future family. I see endless happiness for us— I see children that will grow together, never apart. But life is not always bliss, and I derive the greatest security in knowing that should tragedy rear its ugly head, our future family will know how to deal with that, too, and emerge stronger than before . . .

Tony looked out at the Sound. It was time to go. All of life's celebrations must come to an end—for some, sooner than for others. He picked his way through the guests and retrieved his car in the driveway.

"Leaving so soon, sir?" asked the valet.

"Happy occasions always make me sad."

31

Do you love it, or do you love it? I mean, do you *love* it or do you *love* it?"

"Is there a choice there?"

"Of course, Tony, you blind fuck. What's a question without a choice? That's like a wet nurse without nipples. There's a choice in all my questions. I can't help it if you don't see it."

"I don't."

"I'm asking you, Tony, in which *way* you love it. That should be easy for a smart boy like you. Easy. Do you love this part, because if you don't, who will?"

"I don't like any trials, let alone my own."

"That's being a faggot, if I may say so—and I say that as politely, of course, as if I happened to be a fairy myself. Leave the fairy stuff to the prosecutor. You should love having your head on the block. This is heroic. This is the manly part. This is where I run in with my big, bad Robin

Hood bow and spring you. Do you understand? This is the moment you've been waiting for all your life.

"This is glory. This is heaven, Tony. This is the best in the world. When I see life, I see this part.

"Some people, they see the roses, the birthdays, the dinners over wine, and the engagement rings. I see it for what it is. Which is none of the above. I see it all on my plate. Like a rat turd that no one wants to eat except me. I make it happen and then I enjoy.

"What's with you, Tony? This is your big day. This is fame. This is excitement. This is passion. I know. I know because I live by it. You? You die by it or live by it, depending on the mood I'm in.

"It's like this. Pretend you're the prosecution's star witness. Or better, pretend you're in a movie—you're *the witness for the prosecution*. I know you'll like that. OK, let's say you're a neighbor who saw Tony McMahon's car leaving the Carver estate that night. Let's pretend, OK?"

"OK."

"Good." Barolo looked so content that he didn't need a trial. Life, thought Tony, was kind to this man. He'd never seen himself. "Now, I've got you on the stand. It's cross-examination. You know what that's like, right?"

"Sure. I've seen movies."

"Good. Then we'll play it like the movies. 'Cause the only difference between the movies and the real thing is that the real thing is phony. So I like your movie idea, Tony. You knew I would. Now here goes. You're the weak-hearted neighbor, sixty—a rich widow. Too curious. You saw a car that night—right after you heard what sounded like gunshots. You saw it from your window, high on the hill, you say. You couldn't sleep, and after those gunshots you opened your blinds and you saw a car going down the hill. You were curious—really you're just a nosy bitch—and so you strained your eyes. You couldn't make out much, but you did notice this car driving out of the estate. And that means Carver didn't kill himself. That means there was another person driving out of there. And that means it's Tony. So the idea here, OK, is to nail down the time you heard the car—to nail it down at a time right after the gunshots, so that Tony's cooked.

"So here goes. You play the nosy bitch. I'm going to ask you questions."

"Go ahead."

"You heard a sound that sounded like gunshots?"

"Yes."

"What time was that?"

"It was just after midnight—I woke up and looked at the clock."

"The gunshots woke you?"

"Of course."

"You were awakened suddenly?"

"Yes."

"Let me ask you this. Do you ever have dreams?"

"Of course."

"Do you ever have bad dreams?"

"Yes."

"How often?"

"Occasionally."

"How bad do they get?"

"Quite bad, sometimes."

"What happens in those?"

"Oh, I don't know, I have visions, terrible stuff. Scary things."

"Ever see shapes?"

"Well, of course, the shapes of whatever's in my dreams."

"Ever see people?"

"Again, whatever's in the dreams."

"Ever hear sounds?"

"I don't know."

"You're not sure?"

"How can I know?"

"Well, let me ask it this way. Let's say you have dreams about a baby crying. Would you hear the baby?"

"Well, of course."

"And if you had dreams about a car honking, would you hear the horn?"

"I guess so. Why not?"

"And then if you had dreams about a gun firing, you would hear the gunshots?"

Pause.

"I asked, if you had dreams about a gun firing, would you hear the gunshots?"

"I suppose."

"Then if you'd had a dream about gunshots, you might have heard them in your dreams?"

"Maybe."

"Well then, what you're telling us is, if I can get your answer without leading you along here, is that you could've dreamed those gunshot sounds."

"Maybe."

"And if you dreamed those gunshot sounds, the time you really woke up and looked at the clock could have been an hour later than the time you dreamed those gunshot sounds—or even two hours, or maybe even as many as six?"

Tony sat back in his chair. Playing an old woman had given him a backache.

"You're good, Barolo."

"I'm not good. I'm everything."

32

As in a looking glass, all that's superficial seems realer than real. That scar on your cheek. That seems so present in your reflection. To others it might be an illusion. Or just a part of the scenery. Nothing to write home about. But to you—God—to you, it's everything. It's a reason not to get up in the morning.

See that moon hanging above your head. Really, it's millions of miles away—an optical illusion. It's no closer to your head than the sun is to it. The tricks of life. Reality plays with itself. Reality masturbates.

Reality folds.

That's the problem with reality: It never plays its hand. So it is with everything. What's real is that which never admits to it—that which never says I am what I am. How can we deal with that? How can we deal with the make-believe that tells the truth and the reality that lies to us with smiling teeth?

If you looked at a happy family, as Tony McMahon did—years after the beautiful wedding—you might see a happy life. Or maybe you'd see a happy picture of a life. Or maybe just a picture.

In the photo on the coffee table were two beautiful children in front of a Christmas tree. One was a baby boy, happily nestled in his mother's arms. The other was a little girl, glowing in daddy's embrace. It was a lovely family. The Christmas tree was strung with lights. Presents bulged beneath it. Life seemed to promise something: perhaps a Santa Claus sailing down the chimney.

But certainly not a stranger staring into a strange home. Tony gazed through the leaded panes of the Carver living room and stared at the photo. He'd parked his car at the foot of the Carver drive and listened to the Carver night. He'd hopped the Carver property line and scaled the Carver hill. He'd hurdled the Carver bushes and braved the Carver gardens—and, finally, he'd arrived at the base of the magnificent Carver house.

The photo saddened him. It was so much of what he'd always wanted. Of course, more than anything, it was the woman he wanted.

But it was also the life, the lifestyle. He wanted it all—the presents, the little boy, the little girl, the house, that bureau—this photo. He pictured himself in the husband's place. He could wear that blazer just as easily. He could tilt his head just so slightly, he could sneer just as arrogantly, he could make his daughter glow with joy just as well.

But there was a small sound. And then Tony saw a figure sitting on the couch in the sitting room whom he could barely distinguish through the pale of the moonlight. Looking over the rim of the photo frame, he could hardly make out the form. He looked at the photo and then at the shape and then back again. It was the man of the house. It was Kirk Carver.

But there was something odd about his movements. He was rocking back and forth slowly, as if possessed. He looked only at the floor. He hugged himself.

Then the horror of it struck Tony. It was a sight he'd never seen before. A sight he'd feared since he was young. A sight he'd always feared to find upon coming home from school, between bottles, between nights. It was the agony of a sight—no, the sight itself. It was fearful and awesome. It was the sight of what couldn't really happen. It was the very core of what makes us place photos on coffee tables.

It was the sight of a grown man crying.

Tony started on the way down the hill, back to his car and back into the anonymous night.

33

Dear Charlotte,

My trial begins tomorrow, as I'm sure you've read in some of the papers. By the time you get this note, there might even be a verdict. I've decided that we will be very happy together, if I get out. I thought we could celebrate my freedom by taking a trip to Cape Cod which is a place I've never been to but always wanted to visit. I've always been interested in stories about whales and whaling so it seems like a natural place. If you can think of any better place, let me know. I figured (if I go free) that we could even take a trip across country. I've traveled to many parts of it already and I could show you a few things. If I do get out, the first place I'll go is your place, because I sure don't want to go back to my father's house. The press will probably hang out there anyway and it's time I lived a normal life again. I spend lots of time imagining the things we'll do. I picture us eventually having a big wedding with live music. Now that I'm certified as a minister, maybe I can marry us as well. I know it may be hard for us with my reputation, but eventually I'll find a congregation somewhere and we can settle down. Please tell me your thoughts on these things as soon as you can. I have nothing to do now except wait.

Signed,
Antonio McMahon, Inmate #90245

As he was writing his, she was writing hers:

Dear Tony,

Your trial begins tomorrow so tonight I'll pray for you. I haven't heard from you in some time so I figure you've gotten over me which is good because I've got some bad news to tell you. I'm sorry to tell you that I can't be writing you anymore. Ed found out I was writing you letters and he almost went nuts over it. It took me over a week to calm him down. He got angry like he usually does and it was tough. I know that we probably weren't right for each other in many ways but we did have feelings for each other. When you stopped returning my letters I figured you'd realized you didn't really want anything to do with me. It's just as well. I never felt I deserved any happiness anyway. Ed and I are going to get married in a little bit and then take our honeymoon in Canada where his family comes from. I will pray for you tonight, because I know you are innocent. One thing I became sure of from getting to know you was that you would never hurt anyone. I wish you a safe and happy life.

Signed,
C.

34

Tony's mall shopping list for March 16 read:

- One pair running sneakers
- Three pair Jockey underwear
- Get photos developed
- Cash check
- Camping pack?

While Patricia's read like so:

- Melody's ear medicine
- Melody's birthday present
- Pick up Teddy's photo enlargement
- Kirk's prescription
- Kirk—jogging suit
- Lingerie
- Tampax
- Vitamins

Tony had no real reason to shop at the Hautucket Mall. The Glen River Plaza was much nearer to his father's and had a larger selection of shops. But even the name Hautucket still bewitched him. On a quiet night, he liked to drive through the beautiful winding roads of the Hollow, enjoying the breezes and the quiet. He sometimes came during the day and strained to see his way up the winding drives, around and through the heavy shrubbery, up to the hillsides on which sat the glorious homes. His pilgrimage always ended the same way: with a pass by that particular hill that he knew only by the name on the name plate at its base. He would often sit there, on the shoulder of the road, with the ignition and the lights turned off, and imagine the house and the household. Then he would pull back onto the road and start the drive back to Glen River. That drive back was always filled with the type of loneliness that few people ever recognize for what it is—the type that masquerades as hate or anger or a craving for something inexplicable, and thus hopelessly confuses things.

So the Hautucket Mall was where Tony did his shopping. Though he never seriously entertained the idea of running into Patricia, it gave him a strangely warm feeling that it was a place where she did conceivably shop, or at least where her maid would conceivably shop. But never had he run into anyone he recognized at the Hautucket Mall, let alone Patricia.

Tony liked malls. The myriad of shops and products pleased him. The piped-in Muzak and promotionals didn't bother him one bit. Nor did the bleak decor or fake rock gardens. Far from appearing to him as fake, the mall environment seemed as genuine as anything he had encountered in life. There were no frustrations here. If you wanted a record, you went to the Castle Records. If you desired a slice of pizza, you stopped at the Slice King. If you needed shaving cream, you went to the Pharmart. All requests were provided for and accounted for. In the mall, life finally compensated for its cruel penchant for making people need things.

Since the mall provided such a sense of security for Tony, it disturbed him when the manager told him that his photos would take five days, instead of the usual three, on account of a backlog at the processing plant. He was preparing to stop at the Glen River Plaza on the way home and try the Quik-Photo outlet, when he recognized her hand.

He wasn't sure if it was the texture of the skin or the alignment of the moles and birthmarks, but it was unmistakably hers. Though it was older, it was no bigger than he remembered it. It was cupped in a position he could have sketched from memory. He didn't dare look up at the face for fear that she would recognize him, but he watched her fish in her pocketbook for the photo receipt and hand it over to the manager. That small deed was accomplished with the same quirky elegance that he remembered. She tapped her fingers slightly as she awaited her photos. That, however, was a habit he didn't remember. He supposed married life made some people nervous.

When she retrieved her credit card and turned to leave

the shop, Tony followed her and allowed his gaze to drift up to eye level. She was walking briskly ahead. Deprived of his usual timidity by the intoxication of the encounter, he called out to her:

"Patricia!"

She didn't stop.

"Patricia!" again he called.

She turned on a dime and looked directly in his direction, but her gaze was as quizzical as any could be.

"Yes?" she asked, her voice harsh, questioning, impatient—not like he'd heard it on the surveillance tape that night.

"Antonio McMahon. I'm not sure if you—"

She half smiled. "Of course I do. What a pleasure. But I am in a hurry." She took two steps forward and shook his hand. "It's nice running into you. How's your family? I must be going, really. But it was nice running into you. Take care." And thus she exited with the extraordinarily efficient rebuff mastered at countless cocktail parties and club functions.

Tony stood there, in the center of the hall of the mall where he had shopped so many countless times, and became increasingly aware of the fact that he had no purpose there. People passed on either side of his shoulders and stared at him oddly. There was no better way to explain it. He was a man without a purpose—there, or as he began to fear as he searched for his car in the vast parking lot—anywhere.

35

"What's next for you?"

"See the world, right? Isn't that what I'm supposed to say?"

"How the fuck would I know what you're supposed to say. You could start with *thank you.*"

"Thank you."

"Most of my clients embrace me. You're not the emotional type, are you?"

Tony sat back in his booth. He'd suggested the Porter Hill Diner for the celebratory coffee with Barolo, not because it held any symbolism but because it was a halfway point.

"No. I'm not the emotional type."

"How did it feel for you, though—sitting there and hearing it for yourself? Didn't you feel like the whole fucking ratty world had just turned right side up again."

Tony remembered Charlotte's quote about the world

being turned upside down for some people. It was as though Barolo had finished her verse. "I thought I had something to come out for—something waiting here on the outside. But it fell through. There's really not much here, as it turns out."

"There's sunlight, girls, good food. It's better out here, Tony. Believe me. I make a career on the theory that it's better out here."

"I dreamt in prison every night of being set free. But freedom isn't all it's advertised to be. Just a little more space to roam around in."

"There you go. No big deal. Just the same shitty world waiting for you on the outside. You are a gloomy motherfucker, Tony. You're bad for my sinus condition. I was gonna get a bogus shrink onstage to plead you insanity, but now I think you need a real one."

"Who would've thought you could share everything with your lawyer?"

"Don't even begin to think that. I only take what I need. Don't *ever* give me what I don't ask for."

"Well, what's next for you, counselor?"

"Cases. More cases. You're not the only fucking case, you know. The world doesn't revolve around you, Tony. I got plenty of people that I have to spring loose. And you know what? Most of them pay better than you do."

"Do you want to know what really happened that night. *The* night. I mean, now that all is said and done."

"Tony, every sorry fuck looks for the meaning of life. It's all bullshit. I came out of the womb knowing it was bullshit. If there'd been meaning to life—a truth to it all—my mother would have handed it to me as I slid out from between her legs. Because—rest her soul—she was that kind of woman. So I grew up knowing there was no such thing. All my friends pissed away their life searching for the meaning of it. Where did they end up? In rehab or on some mountaintop dying of dysentery. No, I always knew. That's what kept me sane. So you got nothing to tell me, Tony. No matter what you think you got. When I look at you I see nothing but a free man—no more, no less."

Afterlude

When it snows on the North Shore at Christmastime, it makes for a perfect photo. The elegant suburban homes decked with wreaths and mistletoe speak of good cheer. Wisps of smoke rise gingerly from the chimney tops, and the blanket of whiteness brings quiet to the roads and fields. Hautucket Bay sponsors horse-drawn sleigh rides that wind through the breathtaking passes on the old estates. Children howl with delight as the sleighs careen to and fro on the sharp turns, and parents struggle to keep the bundle of blankets aboard. Christmas parties entice from candlelit living rooms. Delightfully rich eggnog is served up at any number of places. The Crescent Lochs Country Club has well-manicured cross-country ski trails that wind with a supple elegance over knolls and across small ponds. Members like to ski a few miles and then retire for a massage, a sauna and then a hot chocolate on the

South Deck. Over at the Blue Hill Winter Club, skaters circle, spin and fall. Christmas carols play softly over the PA system, and mothers share gossip and tea while nannies mind the children.

In Porter Hill, shoppers rush out of shops and to their cars. Colorful lights and Santa figurines adorn nearly all the display cases. The Christmas Eve expectancy seems to linger for days and days. Pub doors open to allow traces of song to drift into the cold. At Killian's, they serve a special winter ale that cuts through the chill and makes the blood vessels expand nicely. Several gingerbread houses rest on display, awaiting the annual competition. Coats collect in a haphazard mound on the end of the bar. Vincent's closes in December. The door is shuttered tight. A notice reads that they will reopen after New Year's.

The last day of school before Christmas break, a magic possesses the Shore. A child lives for this day. Teachers do, too. Classes barely meet. When they do, Christmas carols are read in lieu of lessons. Everyone wishes everyone well and thinks the New Year will never come. Second graders tote home candy canes with their knapsacks. Fifth graders build snowmen in the parking lot. No one could be happier.

There is, however, something about these days that plagues all of us. Statistically, suicides skyrocket over the holiday season. People become conscious of their loneliness, lost loved ones, and regrets. Domestic violence increases. So do heart attacks. The depression that sets in the first workday after New Year's, when the year commences with no hope of a real respite for many months, is well documented. The frost and the bitter cold that seize the landscape in January have none of December's charm. Cars get stuck and buried in drifts. Engines freeze and crack. Snow turns yellow and brown. People tire of layering and unlayering. Flights to Florida overbook.

It was one of these tired, raw January days, when the holidays have given up and the cold rules without spirit, that Antonio McMahon sat on his couch at his father's house and waited for the reporter to arrive. Three or four newspapers had called him in the weeks following his acquittal. Initially, he'd ignored the phone calls, but some had been more persistent than others. Finally, he'd arranged for an interview with a tabloid.

The reporter scraped his shoes on the welcome mat and rang the bell. He looked around at the sad ranch-style house and waited for the door to open. Again he rang. Finally, a pale face came to the door. The reporter had seen a photo or two of McMahon, but none had prepared him for how simultaneously childish and haggard he would look. Everyone thought the jury had made a serious error with this case. Despite damning forensic evidence, a reasonable doubt had somehow been gleaned from the lawyer's arguments. Now that he saw him for himself, he could only see an awkwardness and timidity ill-equipped for committing murder.

Tony McMahon stepped aside. "Please come in."

"Thank you. You have a nice home. Did you grow up here?"

"I did—with my father. But he passed away ten days ago—"

"I'm sorry, I didn't know. We could—"

Tony waved away his concern. "Please. It wasn't a tragedy."

The reporter took a seat on the bizarre, stained couch. The house was oppressively silent except for the ticking of a grandfather clock and the sound of a tap not fully closed.

"I just have a few questions."

Tony sat across from the reporter on the old E-Z Boy recliner that his father had cherished until he'd taken to spending his day even more horizontal—on the couch. "Go right ahead. I have plenty of time."

"Very well. How has life been treating you since you've been released?"

"Oh, just fine. I have all I want." Tony gestured to the household furnishings. "I don't ask for much."

"And you've found work?"

"Yes. I have a job at South Shore University Hospital. I'm a type of orderly—for the time being."

"You admitted in the trial transcript that you loved Patricia Carver. Do you miss her?"

"I do miss her. I did love her."

"And you were stricken with grief when she was killed?"

Tony smiled. "I was."

"And you never hurt her."

"How could I? She didn't know I existed."

"Never?"

"Never—except of course in grade school—and then maybe later."

"Later? When?"

"When the world turned upside down."

"I beg your pardon?"

Again, Tony smiled. "It's just an expression."

"So, do you think Kirk Carver committed suicide?"

"I have no idea."

"What do you think is the real reason that he would have killed himself? Was Patricia Carver too much to deal with?"

"I'm not sure there is a real reason."

"There's a rumor that you started a pen-pal romance in prison and that you're now engaged?"

A third smile. "That's not true. There was a pen-pal romance, but things didn't work out. There will be a wedding, but I'll be a guest—not the groom. She's marrying her high school sweetheart instead."

"What's her name?"

"Charlotte Celeste . . . a beautiful name, no?"

"Yes, that's a beautiful name. So she still invited you to the wedding anyway? That was gracious of her."

Yet another smile. "Not exactly." Tony pointed at the stack of newspapers in the corner. "The invitation came by way of the wedding announcement in the paper. Let's just say I'll be an uninvited guest."

"Do you think you'll enjoy yourself?"

"I hope so. The last wedding I went to was very nice. On the Sound. A nice band. I like that kind of thing."

"There are some who say that you made a deal with the devil to save yourself from jail. What do you think of that?"

Tony smiled one last time and looked out the window. The reporter followed his gaze but could see nothing but the icy sidewalk and driveway. "There's no question I would've seen fit to deal with the devil. The question is whether the devil would've seen fit to deal with me."

In his dreams he often recalled his beachcomber. The real memories and the fake ones had intertwined so he could never tell the context. Sometimes they were on Jones Beach playing in the waves. Sometimes they were in class together at school. Sometimes there was only blackness, where memory doesn't dare tread. For sometimes there are truths hidden under that blackness. Truths that would only get in the way.